Praise for the Gilded Age Mysteries

Murder in the North End

"[A] unique and enjoyable series . . . The author uses the historical period to great advantage, depicting the class separations and prejudices that existed at the time without romanticizing them. Nell and Will are both fascinating characters. From wholly disparate backgrounds . . . they make a great sleuthing team as well. It's always a good day when a new Nell Sweeney book arrives." —*CA Reviews*

Murder on Black Friday

"The author has an amazing grasp of life during this period of history. Each detail is crafted to let the reader feel immersed in the time; from the major historical events to the minutiae of everyday life. These facts are effortlessly woven into the overall narrative." —*The Romance Readers Connection*

Death on Beacon Hill

"[Nell is] intelligent and has a strong sense of justice . . . She only takes action after careful consideration, never rushing to throw herself in harm's way . . . The mystery consists of several layers and is constructed quite well . . . It's clear from the beginning that things are not as they seem; this serves to keep the reader interested in ferreting out the clues alongside Nell. I'm looking forward to another installment." —*The Romance Readers Connection*

Murder in a Mill Town

"Nell is one of the strongest, most honorable, and dearest heroines to grace the pages of an amateur-sleuth novel . . . P. B. Ryan knows how to write a tale that will grip and keep readers' interest throughout the novel."

—*Midwest Book Review*

RAWN

D0191391

continued . . .

"Ms. Ryan excels in her ability to show her characters' complexities. Most are neither good nor bad, but living lives enmeshed with many shades of gray. Add the rich historical detail and readers have an excellent historical mystery with an intriguing heroine."　　*—The Best Reviews*

"Nell is an interesting and unique character . . . As various elements of her past come to light, it's clear that she is a multilayered character. The mystery itself is done quite well, with clues pointing to various suspects and an unexpected resolution . . . I hope to see much more of Nell in future books."　　*—The Romance Readers Connection*

Still Life with Murder

"What a thoroughly charming book! A beautiful combination of entertaining characters, minute historical research, and a powerful evocation of time and place. I'm very glad there will be more to come."　　—Barbara Hambly,
New York Times bestselling author of *Renfield*

"Utterly absorbing. Vividly alive characters in a setting so clearly portrayed that one could step right into it. A very clever plot in which each clue is clearly offered and yet the identity of the murderer is a complete surprise."
—Roberta Gellis, author of *Chains of Folly*

"*Still Life with Murder* is a skillfully written story of intrigue and murder set during Boston's famous Gilded Age. Nell Sweeney, governess and part-time nurse, is a winning heroine gifted with common sense, grit, and an underlying poignancy. With its rich sense of place and time and a crisp, intelligent plot, readers will speed through this tale and be clamoring for more."　　—Earlene Fowler,
national bestselling author of *Tumbling Blocks*

A BUCKET
OF ASHES

P. B. RYAN

BERKLEY PRIME CRIME, NEW YORK

THE BERKLEY PUBLISHING GROUP
Published by the Penguin Group
Penguin Group (USA) Inc.
375 Hudson Street, New York, New York 10014, USA
Penguin Group (Canada), 90 Eglinton Avenue East, Suite 700, Toronto, Ontario M4P 2Y3, Canada
(a division of Pearson Penguin Canada Inc.)
Penguin Books Ltd., 80 Strand, London WC2R 0RL, England
Penguin Group Ireland, 25 St. Stephen's Green, Dublin 2, Ireland (a division of Penguin Books Ltd.)
Penguin Group (Australia), 250 Camberwell Road, Camberwell, Victoria 3124, Australia
(a division of Pearson Australia Group Pty. Ltd.)
Penguin Books India Pvt. Ltd., 11 Community Centre, Panchsheel Park, New Delhi—110 017, India
Penguin Group (NZ), 67 Apollo Drive, Rosedale, North Shore 0632, New Zealand
(a division of Pearson New Zealand Ltd.)
Penguin Books (South Africa) (Pty.) Ltd., 24 Sturdee Avenue, Rosebank, Johannesburg 2196,
South Africa

Penguin Books Ltd., Registered Offices: 80 Strand, London WC2R 0RL, England

This is a work of fiction. Names, characters, places, and incidents either are the product of the author's imagination or are used fictitiously, and any resemblance to actual persons, living or dead, business establishments, events, or locales is entirely coincidental. The publisher does not have any control over and does not assume any responsibility for author or third-party websites or their content.

A BUCKET OF ASHES

A Berkley Prime Crime Book / published by arrangement with the author

PRINTING HISTORY
Berkley Prime Crime mass-market edition / December 2007

Copyright © 2007 by Patricia Ryan.
Cover art by Maryann Lasher.
Cover design by Rita Frangie.
Interior text design by Kristin del Rosario.

ISBN: 978-0-425-21873-0

BERKLEY® PRIME CRIME
Berkley Prime Crime Books are published by The Berkley Publishing Group,
a division of Penguin Group (USA) Inc.,
375 Hudson Street, New York, New York 10014.
The name BERKLEY PRIME CRIME and the BERKLEY PRIME CRIME design are trademarks of Penguin Group (USA) Inc.

PRINTED IN THE UNITED STATES OF AMERICA

10 9 8 7 6 5 4 3 2 1

For Nick Dichario, Mike Fleming, Rigel Klingman,
Alan Michaels, Karen Van Meenen,
Ben Schaefer, Dan Plumeau,
and all the other, less regular,
Wednesday Night Irregulars,
who help to recharge my batteries
in the middle of the week.
And, of course,
for Suzy,
our Hostess with the Mostest.

I speak of new cities and new people.
I tell you the past is a bucket of ashes.
I tell you yesterday is a wind gone down,
    a sun dropped in the west.
I tell you there is nothing in the world
    only an ocean of to-morrows,
    a sky of to-morrows.

From Carl Sandburg's "Prairie"

Chapter 1

August 1870, Cape Cod, Massachusetts

"MISEENY, who's that man?" asked breathless little Gracie Hewitt as she treaded water in Waquoit Bay flanked by the two young women charged with her care.

"What man, buttercup?" Nell Sweeney, standing waist deep in the placid water, followed Gracie's gaze toward the Hewitts' colossal, cedar-shingled summer "cottage." Shielding her eyes against the late-afternoon sun, she saw a man walking toward them across the vast stretch of lawn that separated the shore from the house. Lean and with a graceful gait, he wore a well-tailored cutaway sack coat and bowler. It wasn't until he removed the bowler and smiled at Nell—that warm, genial smile she'd once known so well—that she recognized him.

"Oh, my word," Nell murmured.

"Who is he, then?" asked Eileen Tierney in her softly girlish brogue.

"He's, um, someone I used to know when I lived here on the Cape. I haven't seen him for some time."

It had been three years since Nell, who lived in Boston with the Hewitts except for summers here at Falconwood, had last crossed paths with Dr. Cyril Greaves. In July of 'sixty-seven, she had accompanied her employer, Viola Hewitt, to a charity tea in Falmouth, and he'd been there. Their conversation had been cordial—affectionate, even—but as if by unspoken agreement, neither had made any move to resume their acquaintance. Two summers before that, they'd passed each other on Short Street in Falmouth, he in his all-weather physician's coupé and Nell and Gracie in their little Boston chaise, and had chatted for a minute until a salt wagon rumbling up behind Dr. Greaves had forced him to move on.

For him to actually seek her out this way was unusual enough to be disconcerting.

"Och, but he's a handsome fella," whispered Eileen.

"He's married," Nell said. "And he's older than he seems."

The first time Nell had seen Dr. Greaves, she was struck by his resemblance to a statue of St. Francis of Assisi in front of St. Catherine's, her parish church. Born with patrician good looks, expressive eyes, and that ready smile, he was further blessed by being one of those lucky men who didn't seem to age much in their middle years. His light brown hair had but a whisper of gray at the temples, and he still moved like a man in his twenties.

"Is he nice?" Gracie panted, switching to a dog paddle to keep up with Nell as she waded toward shore.

"He is very nice."

"Can I meet him?"

"*Can* you?"

"*May* I?" asked the child with a put-upon roll of the eyes.

"You *have* met him. You just don't remember."

"I'd like to meet him again."

Nell paused at the edge of the bay to wring out the sodden, knee-length skirt of her bathing costume as Dr. Greaves crossed the sandy stretch of beach. She looked up to find him taking in her attire—the puffy cap, black wool sailor dress, matching pantaloons, and lace-up slippers—with a contemplative smile that made her cheeks bloom with heat.

"Oh, do stop gaping at me," she said through a flutter of embarrassed laughter.

"Is that any way to greet an old friend?"

Old friend. Curious, Nell thought, that Dr. Greaves should refer to himself that way. Much as they'd cared for each other, they'd never been *friends*, precisely; certainly she'd never thought of them as such.

"And I wasn't gaping," he said. "I was admiring." Before Nell could summon a reply to that, he turned to greet Gracie and Eileen with a bow. "Ladies. So sorry to intrude upon you unannounced like this, but the butler told me you were out here, and that I should just come on back."

"Quite right," Nell said. "Grace Hewitt, Eileen Tierney, may I present Dr. Cyril Greaves, a physician from East Falmouth." To Dr. Greaves, she said, "Miss Tierney helps me to look after Gracie, with whom you are already acquainted."

"I'm most pleased to see you again, Miss Hewitt," said Dr. Greaves.

"And I you," said Gracie, the consummate little Brahmin lady in her short white bathing dress and damp braids.

The child's decorous reply drew an impressed grin from Dr. Greaves. "I must say, that is a much more mannerly salutation than the red-faced squalls with which you greeted me the first time we met."

"Dr. Greaves is the physician who took you out of your mommy's tummy," Nell told Gracie.

"With Miss Sweeney's help," he said. "I couldn't have done it without her." A gracious statement, indeed, for it was he and he alone who had saved both Gracie's life and that of her mother, a chambermaid named Annie McIntyre, by means of a deft and timely Cesarean section that storm-ravaged night six years ago. Meeting Nell's gaze, he said, "I should never have let her go."

Looking up at Nell, eyes wide, Gracie said, "You were there when I was born?"

She hesitated. Dr. Greaves winced, evidently realizing he'd just revealed something that Nell, in an effort to forestall Gracie's incessant questions about her parentage, had kept to herself. With the cat out of the bag, Nell nodded and said, "I was Dr. Greaves's assistant for four years. Then, after you arrived and Nana decided to adopt you, she asked me if I would come to Boston to be your nursery governess."

But not before questioning Dr. Greaves, in a conversation overheard by Nell, as to her suitability to care for and tutor a young girl. *She's of good character and chaste habits, I take it?* His response had been reassuring, if purposefully vague. There'd been no hint—thank God, because Nell had desperately wanted the position—of her disreputable past, nor of the fact that she'd been sharing the lonely doctor's bed for three of the four years in which she'd lived under his roof.

From a good family, is she? Mrs. Hewitt had asked him.

They were from the old country, ma'am. Both gone now, first him and then the mother, when Nell was just a child.

And there's no other family?

She had a number of younger siblings—that's how she learned to care for children. Disease took most of them—cholera, diphtheria—but one brother lived to adulthood. She assumes he's still alive, but it's been years since she's seen him. James—she calls him Jamie.

Nell had let out the breath she'd been holding, weak with relief and gratitude that he hadn't mentioned Duncan. The rest of it was damning enough, but if Viola had known about Duncan, there would have been no question of hiring her.

Naturally, Viola had told Nell when she offered her the position, *I would prefer that you remain unwed while Grace is young, in order to devote your full attention to her. And of course, your conduct and reputation must be above reproach—you're responsible for the upbringing of a young girl, after all. But I can't think you'd let me down in that regard.*

If Nell had managed, these past six years, to live up to Viola's expectations, it was only by perpetuating a lie of omission to a woman she'd come to regard as a surrogate mother. As far as Viola knew—then and now—Miss Nell Sweeney was a virtuous Irish Catholic girl from a working-class background who was good with children. There'd been so much Nell had been obliged to keep hidden all these years, lest she risk the loss of her position, her wonderful new life, and most unthinkable of all, Gracie.

"Miseeny?" Gracie was tugging at her skirt. "*Did* you?"

"Did I what, sweetie?"

"Know my mommy? My weal mommy? *Real*," she added, correcting herself before Nell could.

"I had never met her before that night," Nell answered truthfully.

"Did *you*?" she asked Dr. Greaves.

He shook his head. "I'm sorry, no."

Nell said, "Gracie, you know what Nana says. She'll tell you about your mommy as a birthday present when you turn twelve."

Although the child was equally curious about her father, there had been, at his insistence, no such promise to reveal his identity. Recently Gracie had overheard Mrs. Mott, the housekeeper, say that she'd been "sired by a Hewitt," and had pressed Nell as to what that meant. In response, Nell had uttered the only outright lie she'd ever told the child: " 'Sired' means adopted. Mrs. Mott was talking about Nana's having picked you out special because she'd always wanted a little girl."

Eileen, adept at changing the subject when it veered down this particular path, said to Dr. Greaves,

"You'd be the one, then, that taught Miss Sweeney nursing."

"More than just nursing," Nell said. "He taught me arithmetic, French, history, music, comportment . . . I didn't even know how to write a proper letter till Dr. Greaves got hold of me." He'd been her Pygmalion, she his grateful Galatea.

"Nell had an extraordinarily quick mind," Dr. Greaves told Eileen. Eyeing the delicate, flaxenhaired nineteen-year-old with keen interest, he said, "Forgive me, Miss Tierney, but have we met?"

"I don't figger we could of, sir. I only been in this country two years, and I never set foot on the Cape till this summer."

"You look familiar, but perhaps I'm just confusing you with someone else." Dr. Greaves turned to Nell. "I, er, wonder if I might have a word with you." He glanced at Gracie and Eileen. "Perhaps we could take a walk?"

"You go ahead, Miss Sweeney," said Eileen. "I'll take Gracie back to the house and get her washed up and fed."

Nell and Dr. Greaves strolled in silence along the beach toward a handsome edifice adjacent the

Hewitts' private dock, built half on land and half on stone pilings in the water. Like the estate's main house, it was cedar-shingled, with slate-roofed gables, a turret, and a veranda overlooking the bay, from which stairs descended to the dock. The ground level, which was open to the bay and fitted out with two boat slips, housed a small sailboat, a rowboat, a canoe, and a pair of sleek shells. Above that was a guest suite.

"So that's the famous Falconwood boathouse, eh?" asked Dr. Greaves as they neared it. "They say it's the grandest on the Cape. Mr. Hewitt sails, I take it?"

"Not anymore," said Nell, knowing that Dr. Greaves hadn't come here to talk about the boathouse, and wondering why he was stalling; he wasn't the type of man to beat about the bush. "Martin, the youngest son, takes one of the shells out a couple of times a day when he's here, as long as the weather's amenable. He's out there right now."

"Martin, he was the pious one, yes?"

Nell nodded. "He's a minister at King's Chapel now. His first sermon was right before I left Boston, and it was brilliant. I can't remember when I've been so moved."

"A devout Catholic like you, attending a Unitarian service? That must be good for an extra few eons in Purgatory."

"Actually . . . I've been attending services at King's Chapel for some time now."

Dr. Greaves stopped in his tracks at the side of the house where the dock began. "You're joking."

"Now you really *are* gaping at me."

"*You? A Protestant*?"

"It's a long story."

Dr. Greaves gestured toward the sixty-foot dock, which terminated in a large raised platform set up with lounging furniture, and offered his arm. "Shall we?" As he escorted her down the narrow plank walkway, he said, "The other son was more of a rogue, as I recall. Squirmed out of joining the Army during the war . . . Henry?"

"Yes, but they call him Harry, and 'rogue' is a very polite term for what he is. He's not the only other Hewitt son, though. There's the eldest, William."

"But I thought William died at Andersonville, during the war, he and the next eldest, Robert. I'm sure that's what we were told that night we delivered Gracie."

"Robbie died. Will escaped, but it took him years

to reunite with his family." Not that he was ever "reunited," precisely, with the rigid and judgmental August Hewitt, who couldn't bear the sight of him—or of Nell, for that matter.

"William—he was the one who earned his medical degree at Edinburgh?"

"Yes, he was brought up with relatives in England, but he came back here when war was declared and enlisted in the Union Army as a battle surgeon."

"Did he establish a practice after the war?"

Nell chose her words carefully, lest Dr. Greaves conclude, as had August Hewitt, that Will was a reprobate of the first water. "He hasn't practiced medicine since then—although he treated Eileen for her clubfoot last year."

"Your assistant? She doesn't have a clubfoot."

"Not anymore. Will arranged for a famous orthopedic surgeon from New York to come to Boston and operate on her."

Dr. Greaves snapped his fingers. "*That's* where I know her from. Louis Albert Sayre was the surgeon—brilliant man. I watched that operation in the surgical theater at Massachusetts General."

Nell was going to say something about his professional dedication in coming all the way up to

Boston from the Cape when she recalled that he made that trip every week or two to visit his beloved wife, Charlotte, who'd been a psychiatric patient at Mass General since well before the war.

"Eileen does wear special, custom-made boots," Nell said, "but she hardly limps anymore. Will was very pleased with the outcome."

"If he hasn't been practicing medicine since the war," Dr. Greaves asked, "what *has* he been doing?"

Gambling and weaning himself off opiates. "He taught medical jurisprudence at Harvard one semester," she said. "His closest friend, Isaac Foster, is assistant dean of the medical school, and he's issued Will a standing offer of a full professorship so that he can develop a forensics curriculum, but there's a catch. Will would have to sign a five-year contract, and he's . . . not comfortable with that kind of commitment."

"Not comfortable with a full professorship at Harvard Medical School?" Dr. Greaves asked incredulously.

Stepping up onto the platform, Nell turned to look out over the water, her arms wrapped around herself. "Will is a . . . complicated man. And, too, he'd had another offer. President Grant wrote him last month, when France and Prussia started mobilizing for war. Our ambassador to France, Elihu Washburne, was asking for a good field surgeon. The president had met Will several times during the war, and he came away with a very high opinion of him."

"A field surgeon? But we're not allied with France in that war. We're entirely neutral."

"Mr. Washburne isn't, and he's resolved to remain in Paris and do what he can to aid France, never mind that it's utter bedlam there now. Will accepted the position."

"Why would any American in his right mind risk life and limb in a fight that isn't ours, that isn't even particularly righteous? It's just so much chest-beating between Napoleon and Wilhelm."

"He had his reasons," said Nell, thinking of the letter Will had left on her pillow the night before he took ship, three and a half weeks ago. *You will wonder why I've chosen this course, rather than the more comfortable alternative of teaching at Harvard. We have reached a juncture in the path of our acquaintance, you and I, from whence we cannot continue as before, strolling along side by side with no particular destination in mind, at least none of which we dare speak . . .*

"Is he to remain in Paris," asked Dr. Greaves, "or provide medical service in the field?"

"The latter. Last week he cabled me from Paris to say that he would be leaving the next day to serve Napoleon's army." *Am to join Marshal MacMahon's I Corps near Wissembourg on German border and remain with them for duration of war. Unable to write for some time, perhaps months. Please do not worry, and ask same of Mother and Martin.*

"He cabled *you*?"

"We've . . . become friendly over the past couple of years."

Dr. Greaves was studying her in that all too insightful way of his. "When is he to return?"

"Not until the war ends. He told me it could be months from now, or—" Her throat closed up around the word "years."

"Ah."

"What was it that you wanted to talk to me about, Dr. Greaves?"

He nodded toward a pair of wicker rocking chairs. "Let's sit."

She lowered herself into the chair he held steady for her, and then he turned the other chair to face hers. He sat forward with his elbows on his knees and expelled a lingering sigh. "A young woman was brought to me this morning for medical treatment. A girl, really—nineteen, but a young nineteen. Claire Gilmartin is her name. She lives with her widowed mother on the outskirts of East Falmouth. They have a little cranberry farm on Mill Pond. You remember Mill Pond, just to the west of the village?"

"Of course," said Nell, rocking absently.

"Claire had grown hoarse and developed a wheezing cough that morning, with dark sputum. She seemed a bit mentally confused as well, but that may have just been her. There was no mystery as to the cause of her malady. One of their outbuildings— they called it a cranberry shed—had burned down the night before last, and Claire had been trapped in it for a little while before she managed to escape."

"This happened, what—thirty-six hours before, and she'd only just started coughing this morning?"

"The symptoms of smoke inhalation can take that long to develop. In any event, it appears that a man unknown to them had gotten caught in the fire and died. Yesterday, when the ashes and debris were cleared away, his remains were removed and taken to Falmouth for assessment by the county coroner.

According to Mrs. Gilmartin, he was one of those two men the police have been looking for, the ones who shot that woman in the beach house."

"I'm sorry," Nell said. "I don't have any idea what you're talking about. We're really rather isolated here."

"You don't read the *Barnstable Patriot*, I see. Do you get the Boston papers, or do without altogether when you're summering here?"

"Mr. Hewitt brings the Boston papers when he comes down for the weekends, but we get the *New York Herald* every day, and that's what I've been reading. It comes on the train from New York. Brady, the Hewitts' driver, goes to Falmouth and gets it."

"Every day? That's almost an hour's drive each way."

"It's because of the war, and Will being over there. Mrs. Hewitt wants to keep apprised of all the new developments—as do I, of course."

"Understandable—as is your lack of interest in local doings, I suppose, given that you're only here for summer relaxation. But to those of us who live here year-round, the Cunningham incident was big news. It happened a couple of weeks ago. Susannah

Cunningham was shot dead by burglars in her home—one of those huge new summer palaces in Falmouth Heights."

"How awful."

"The burglars got away, albeit empty-handed, and the Falmouth constabulary has spent the past two weeks searching for them. There'd been some evidence that they were still in the area, in hiding."

"One of them in the Gilmartins' cranberry shed," Nell said.

Dr. Greaves nodded. "The body was identified last night. Mrs. Gilmartin told me his name and said it would be in the *Patriot* today. It comes out on Thursdays, but they're issuing an extra. I didn't want you to read about it without being prepared." Dr. Greaves gentled his voice, his expression bleak. "I hate to have to tell you this. She said his name was James Murphy."

Nell stopped rocking. She stared at Dr. Greaves.

"I'm so sorry, Nell." He reached over to squeeze her hand.

"How . . . how do they know it was him if he'd . . . if he'd been burned? Wouldn't he have been . . . ?"

"I don't know. I only know what Mrs. Gilmartin told me."

"Are you sure it was Jamie?" she asked. "Murphy is such a common name. So is James."

"I suppose," he said, but she could tell he was humoring her. "Have you been in touch with your brother at all these past . . . ?"

"No, not since he was sent to prison for robbing that livery driver in 'fifty-nine. The first time I came to visit him, he told me not to come again, that he didn't want any visitors, even me. I did come again, but he wouldn't see me. I wrote to him after Duncan was arrested, to let him know what had happened, and that I was living at your house, but he never wrote back. Of course, he wasn't much for writing, but I think he could have managed a short note—something."

"How long was his sentence, again?"

"Eighteen months. I thought perhaps he would look me up after he was released, but he didn't. I began to worry that perhaps he'd been killed by another prisoner, or caught some disease in there, so I wrote to the superintendent of the Plymouth House of Corrections—remember? You helped me to compose the letter."

"Oh yes, I remember."

"He wrote back saying that Jamie had been

released in May of 'sixty-one. I never heard from him again. He was fed up with me and my preaching about how he should live his life. Who could blame him, especially considering how I was living mine at the time. A classic case of the pot calling the kettle black." Nell had often wondered, this past decade, what had become of the ne'er-do-well younger brother who was her last remaining sibling, the rest having succumbed before they'd made it to adolescence. Jamie's likeliest fate, she'd supposed, would have been another prison term. She'd thought that was the worst it would come to.

"Nell?"

Nell realized she'd been staring dully at the opposite shore of the bay. She should be crying, she should be consumed with grief, but she had the most curious sensation of being wrapped in cotton wool. The brick wall of respectability she'd built around herself since moving to Boston had served to insulate her from a past tainted by poverty and pestilence and vice, a past of which Jamie had been an integral part. In the interest of self-preservation, she'd cultivated an emotional distance from everything she'd been and done during the first eighteen years of her life, everyone she'd known—even her own brother. Now, it was as if someone were taking a sledgehammer to that protective wall, trying to bash a hole in it.

Gripping the arms of her chair, she went to rise from it, forgetting that it was a rocking chair. It swayed, and she with it, the blood draining from her head so fast that she nearly keeled over. No doubt she would have, had Dr. Greaves not caught her up and eased her back down onto the chair.

"Relax," he said, pressing gently on her head to lower it. "That's right. Take deep breaths."

"I'm all right," she said, feeling starved for air. "I just . . . it's just this blasted heat."

"And this awful news, I should imagine."

"Yes, of course," she said.

"We'll stay here till you've got your bearings," he said, "and then I'll walk you back to the house."

"Do you remember the first time you saw this house, that night we came here to deliver Gracie?" asked Dr. Greaves as he escorted Nell by the arm onto the back porch, one of four ringing the palatial house. She knew that the purpose of his patter, which he'd kept up during the walk from the beach to the house, was to keep her mind off Jamie. It was the same trick he used, and had taught her to use, to keep patients calm. "You called it a castle. You couldn't believe the Hewitts only spent six weeks a year here."

"You told me it had over twenty rooms," said Nell, trying to shake off the numb shock that gripped her. "There are actually forty, if you count the servants' rooms and nurseries on the third floor."

"Nell?" came a woman's British inflected voice. "Is that you?"

They entered the vast and opulent great hall to find Viola Hewitt sitting in her wheelchair, silhouetted by the sunlight streaming in through the two-story bay window on the back wall.

"Mrs. Hewitt," Nell said, "do you remember Dr. Greaves?"

"How could I forget?" Viola wheeled toward them, guiding the chair around a pair of leather-upholstered settees flanking the monumental fireplace. Between them was a sheepskin rug on which Gracie's little red poodle, Clancy, lay curled up asleep. "Our Gracie might not have survived that night without you. How very lovely to see you again, Dr. Greaves," she said as she extended her hand.

"The pleasure is all mine. I must say, Mrs. Hewitt, you've changed very little these past six years. You are quite as handsome a lady now as you were then."

Idle flattery it may have been, but it was also the simple truth. The tall, angular Viola Hewitt, with her silver-threaded black hair and serene eyes, was the most striking woman Nell had ever met. Of her four sons, the only one who resembled her was Will. Martin, Harry, and the late Robbie were fair, like their father.

Viola was dressed this afternoon in one of the flowing, silken tea gowns she favored for daytime wear, her throat circled by a hefty turquoise necklace from Mexico that few other Brahmin matrons would deign to wear. On her lap was the silver mail tray from the hallstand by the front door, which held an envelope and an unfolded letter.

"Will you stay for supper, Dr. Greaves?" Viola asked.

"I wish I could, but I have some patients to visit this afternoon, so I must be on my way."

"You must join us Friday, then. I'm giving a little dinner to celebrate the return of my son Harry and his new bride from Europe. They're in Boston now, but they've decided to spend a few days here with us. Mr. Hewitt will be coming down with them on the train for the weekend, and my son Martin will still be here. He doesn't have to return to Boston until Saturday."

"What a kind invitation, Mrs. Hewitt," he said. "I believe I would enjoy that, especially if Nell can join us."

"Why not? Eileen can feed Gracie her supper that night. And please call me Viola. I'm really not very keen on formality."

"Then you must call me Cyril." Turning to Nell with a smile, he said, "Both of you."

Nell wasn't quite sure how to respond to the implied shift in their acquaintanceship. "I don't know if I could get used to that. Old habits, you know."

"Do try," he said. "It would please me."

Nell walked him through the entry hall and onto the front porch, whereupon he touched her arm, saying quietly, "Are you going to be all right?"

"It doesn't seem real. Maybe it isn't. Maybe it wasn't even Jamie. If only there were some way to find out for sure."

"I would imagine it was the police who identified him," he said. "If you'd like, I can take you to see the Falmouth chief constable tomorrow. He's got jurisdiction over East Falmouth. You can ask him how he made the identification—if Gracie can spare you for a few hours."

"Eileen can look after Gracie. I *would* like to talk to the constable. It's very kind of you to offer, Dr. Gr—Cyril."

He smiled. "See? That wasn't so hard, was it?"

He told her he would come by for her at ten the next morning, and took his leave.

"I know it may be none of my affair," said Viola as Nell rejoined her, "but it's clear you're troubled. Is it anything you'd care to talk about?"

"It's . . . about my brother Jamie," Nell said. "Or someone with the same name, but . . . that's probably wishful thinking."

Viola looked a little surprised that Nell had brought up the subject of her brother, as well she might. Nell never spoke about Jamie, nor had she ever corrected Viola's assumption that they'd had a falling-out years before. How else to explain an estrangement of eleven years that was due not so much to ill feelings as to Jamie's disinclination to have anything to do with her? And what was Nell supposed to answer, should Viola ask her what her brother did for a living? *He's been a petty criminal since he was a child, mostly sneak thievery, robbing drunks, and holding up carriages on out-of-the-way roads. And picking pockets, which, as a matter of fact, happened to be a particular talent of mine.*

"Has your brother been in contact?" Viola asked.

Nell shook her head, looking down. "He . . . Dr. Greaves thinks he's been killed. In a fire."

"Oh, my dear." Viola wheeled closer and grabbed Nell's hand. "Oh, what dreadful news. I am so terribly, terribly sorry."

"I . . . I still don't quite believe it. I don't think I will until I speak to this constable tomorrow."

Folding up the letter in her hand, Viola said, "This can wait, then."

"What is it?" Nell asked.

"It's nothing. It's not important, not now, while you have so much on your mind."

Nell's gaze lit on the envelope lying faceup on the silver tray. Reading it upside down, she saw that it was addressed to *Mr. and Mrs. August Hewitt* in a strained, almost juvenile hand. Her mouth flew open when she saw the name on the return address: *Chas. A. Skinner.*

"That's from Detective Skinner? Why on earth

would he write to *you*?" asked Nell. "He barely knows you."

"It's not 'Detective' anymore, remember? It's not even 'Constable.' "

"Of course. It's just force of habit to call him that. Loathsome little weasel."

Charlie Skinner, once a member of the elite but defunct Boston Detectives Bureau, had been downgraded at the beginning of this year to uniformed patrolman on the weight of his corruption and myriad misdeeds. Unwilling to accept that this demotion was his own doing—his type never was—he blamed Nell's friend, State Detective Colin Cook. So virulent was his hatred of the Irish detective that he plotted to get Cook convicted of a murder he hadn't committed. The scheme turned against him, though, thanks in large part to Nell and Will, and last month he was booted off the force altogether.

"What did he write to you?" Nell asked.

Choosing her words with evident care, Viola said, "Mr. Skinner obviously harbors a great deal of anger toward you for being the instrument of his downfall. It's nothing you need trouble yourself over during this difficult—"

"Mrs. Hewitt," Nell said quietly. "Viola. Please."

Viola looked from Nell to the letter, grim-faced. "Have a seat, my dear," she said, nodding toward the nearest settee.

"My bathing dress is wet. I don't want to get—"

"Sit, Nell."

Chapter 2

NELL sat, shivering in her damp swimming clothes. Viola unfolded the letter and handed it to her.

Boston
Friday, July 29, 1870

My Dear Sir and Madame,
*   You will no doubt wonder why I who am barely aquainted with you have penned this missive. By way of explanation may I explain that*

*until recentley, which is to say the 9th of July, I
was employed by the City of Boston as a Constable, a fact which is known to Mrs. Hewitt who
may regard me ill but who I pray will credit the
contents of this missive. In the days preceding
my termination I was engaged in inquiries pur-
suant to my Constabulary duties, which inquiries were thwarted hammer and tongs by the
ill-advised labors of the Irish female who you
employ as a governess, in concequence of which
I was as I say relieved of my duties.*

*As I am led to understand that you hold the
highest regard for Miss Sweeney, who is no
"miss" as I shall explain—*

Looking up sharply, Nell saw Viola sitting in
front of the bay window with her back to the room,
gazing out onto the exquisitely landscaped north
lawn and the bay to the east. Nell returned her attention to the letter, her hands shaking so badly that
she could barely focus on the words.

*As I am led to understand that you hold the
highest regard for Miss Sweeney, who is no
"miss" as I shall explain, it falls to me as a man*

of rectitude who is vexed to see good folks such as yourselves gulled by a cunning Colleen to inform you that "Miss" Sweeney is in no way what she appears to be. On the 8th of July in the course of my afore-mentioned duties I had ocassion to observe "Miss" Sweeney leave your home on Tremont St. and hire a hackney coach, her uneasy manner arousing my intrest to the degree that I followed her at a distance in my gig North across the river to Charlestown.

The hack proceeded to Charlestown State Prison, the driver waiting outside the gate as "Miss" Sweeney entered the Prison where she remained from one o'clock in the afternoon until half passed that hour. When she came out and got back in the hack I could not help but notice that her color was high and her atire unkempt withal. Which is to say her hat being crooked and a fair degree of dust besmirching the back of her dress.

You can imagine my cogitations as to what such a visit might betoken. Upon finding myself two days thence in posession of considerable free time I set about making inquiries as to the nature of that visit. Such inquiries being hindered by my being sacked and the stain upon my

*repute it took me some time to sort things out.
But at length I became privy to the truth, which
is that "Miss" Sweeney is MRS. Sweeney wife of
Duncan Sweeney inmate at Charlestown State
Prison these 10 years passed with 20 more years
to serve for the crimes of armed robbery and ag-
gravated assault.*

*Knowing that good folks such as yourselves
could not and would not countenance such bald
DECIET I took pen to paper so that you might
know how you have been hoodwinked and act
accordingly, which is to say sack MRS. Sweeney
with all haste. I warrant she is as Bad an Apple
as ever washed up on our shores.*

*Ever most faithfully yours,
Chas. A. Skinner*

Nell lowered the letter, sweat beading coldly on
her face. *Please, St. Dismas. Please don't let this
happen. I can't lose her. I can't lose Gracie.*

She pressed a hand to her stomach as it pitched,
launching a surge of bile into her throat. "Oh, God."

Bolting up from the settee, she raced through the
buttery and down the service hallway to the little

bathroom off the laundry room, hunched over the water closet, and emptied her stomach. She flushed, rinsed out her mouth, and surveyed herself in the toilet glass. Her face was waxen, her eyes panicky. She whipped the absurd bathing cap off her head, and with palsied hands smoothed down her hair, plaited into a single, still damp, rusty brown braid.

"God, help me," she whispered, and walked back to the great hall on legs that felt as if they were made of India rubber.

Viola was sitting with the letter in her hand, watching Nell gravely; Clancy, sitting next to her, bore a similar expression. "Are you quite all right?"

Nell nodded, although, of course, she was anything but. "It's the heat," she said dully as she wiped her forehead with the back of her arm. "This blasted heat."

"And this letter, I should think. From your reaction . . . It's true, I take it."

Nell sank to her knees in front of Viola, her strength utterly sapped by the double volley of bad news in such a brief period of time. "I'm sorry, Mrs. Hewitt," she said in a watery voice. "I'm sorry. I . . . I never meant to deceive you. That is, I never wanted to. I hated it, I always hated it. But I just . . . I knew I couldn't be Gracie's governess if I was married, especially to a . . . to someone like Duncan."

"Does Will know?" Viola asked. All she knew about Nell and Will was that they'd developed a friendship based on common interests, not the least of which was Gracie. When people had started whispering about the amount of time they were spending together, they pretended to be engaged in order to protect Nell's reputation. Viola knew about the bogus engagement, as did her husband, but she had no notion of the true extent of their relationship.

"He knows," Nell said. "And Dr. Greaves. And of course, Father Gannon at St. Stephen's. And Father Donnelly at St. Catherine's in East Falmouth. He was my confessor before I moved to Boston. No one other than them."

Viola sat back in her chair, nodding pensively, her gaze on the letter.

"Mrs. Hewitt . . ." Nell said, swallowing down the urge to burst into tears. Viola, with her classic British restraint, disdained emotional outbursts. "Gracie means everything to me. I couldn't give her up. I'd rather die."

Viola stared at Nell, and then her expression softened, and she said, "Oh, Nell. Oh, my dear." Leaning down, she stroked Nell's cheek with her cool, soft hand. "You think I'm going to dismiss you? How poorly you know me."

"But . . . Mr. Hewitt, when he reads that letter . . ."

Through a little gust of laughter, Viola said, "Mr. Hewitt is never going to read this letter."

She spun her chair around, plucked a match safe off a console table, and wheeled over to the fireplace. Scraping aside the summer screen of stained glass, she tossed the letter and envelope onto the empty grate, lit a match, and threw it in. Within about two minutes, all that was left of Charlie Skinner's damning "missive" were some flakes of black, papery ash.

"Here, let me get that," Nell said as Viola went to replace the heavy screen. Pulling it back over the hearth, she said, "I . . . I don't know how to thank you, Mrs. Hewitt. I *am* sorry for having misled you, dreadfully sorry."

"Well, I mean, obviously I would have preferred that you'd been candid with me, but looking back, it wasn't really outright deception. I assumed from the beginning that you were unwed. You simply never corrected me."

"You're being generous, Mrs. Hewitt. I did call myself *Miss* Sweeney. I'd stopped calling myself

'Mrs.' ever since Duncan . . . well, ever since he went to prison. I've worried for six years about what would happen if it became known that I was married to a convict. I'm truly humbled by your kindness and your understanding."

"Do sit down, my dear. You're so very pale."

Mindful of her damp clothes, Nell sat on the edge of the hearth.

"I *ought* to be understanding," Viola said. "I've a skeleton rattling 'round in my own closet, after all."

Nell was one of two people, Mr. Hewitt being the other, who knew that at the time of the Hewitts' wedding, Viola was some five months pregnant by the French painter Emil Toussaint. During a calculatedly lengthy European honeymoon, Viola gave birth to Will, whom August had never been able to accept as his own, despite his well-meaning assurances to that effect when he proposed to Viola.

"But to be quite frank," Viola continued, "had I known about Duncan six years ago, I can't say it wouldn't have given me pause, not just because your husband was in prison, but because you *had* a husband. I was concerned about your attention being divided while Gracie was young. As it turned out," she said with a wry smile, "your husband's imprisonment ensured that you were able to devote yourself fully to Gracie."

"I love her as if she were my own. For the longest time, I thought I'd never . . ." *Careful.* Viola was tolerant and indulgent, remarkably so, but there would be a limit to how much even she could accept. "I thought I'd never have a child to love and care for, but now I have Gracie, and she means the world to me."

"You needn't discuss this if you don't want to," Viola said. "It's really none of my affair, after all, but I can't help but wonder why a fine young woman such as yourself would, well . . ."

"Get involved with the criminal?" With a cheerless smile, Nell said, "Don't think I haven't asked myself that same question many times. The thing is, I didn't realize what he was when I first met him. My . . . my brother Jamie introduced us. He brought Duncan around to the poor house to meet me, and—"

"Poor house?" said Viola, obviously aghast.

Nell lowered her gaze to her hands, twisting the hem of her bathing dress as if to wring it out. "The Barnstable County Poor House. I hadn't wanted you to know. I felt . . . well, I was ashamed, of course, but I was also worried that if you knew how I'd grown up, you'd consider me unsuitable to be a governess."

"I don't judge people by their backgrounds, but by who they are—though I must say, your having turned out so well after enduring such an upbringing speaks well for your character. Did you live there for your entire childhood?"

Nell shook her head. "Only from the age of eleven. Before that, I lived in East Falmouth. My father was a day laborer on the docks, when he was working. But he was a drunk, and he abandoned us. A year later my mother died of cholera, along with one of my sisters and two of my brothers."

"Oh, Nell."

"Another sister had died three years before— some lung ailment, I'm not really sure what it was. So that left Jamie and Tess and me. Jamie was a year and a half younger than I, and Tess was just an infant, a newborn. We were sent to the poor house, which was . . ." Nell shook her head, her eyes closed. "You can't imagine."

"I've done charity work in those places, remember? I can imagine all too well."

"At least I had Tess to take care of, and that gave me the sense that God had a plan for me, that I wasn't just a charity case, that I was doing something worthwhile. She was the sweetest little thing, Tess, with big, dark eyes, just like Gracie. But, um . . ." Nell took a deep, shaky breath. "She died of diphtheria when she was just shy of her fourth birthday."

Viola closed her eyes with a pained expression.

Nell looked away from her so as to stifle her urge to weep. "Jamie ran off then, said he had enough of being a ward of the state, and that he was going to make his own way from now on, never mind he was just twelve. I was tempted to leave, too, but a girl my age on her own . . . I'd seen enough unwed mothers come and go through those doors to know how it would have turned out."

"A wise decision, I should think. The better of two evils."

"Jamie used to sneak back in to visit me, and one day a couple of years later, when I was sixteen, he brought Duncan, who was eighteen at the time. I was at a low point then, despondent, listless. I had been ever since I lost Tess, because I blamed myself for not having been able to save her. Duncan . . . he was like this shining god, beautiful, charming, utterly magnetic. He made *me* feel beautiful. He made me feel worthwhile. And he gave me a way to escape from the poor house without ending up walking the streets. He asked me to marry him just a month and a half after meeting me. I was thrilled. I thought my trials were over," she said, a bitter edge creeping into her voice.

"I take it he wasn't the savior you'd thought he would be."

"He wasn't—isn't—a monster, but he was just a small-time thief, like Jamie." And like her, eventually, though it had been Duncan who'd coerced her into it. "And he was an ugly drunk, very ugly."

It was clear from Viola's expression that she knew what Nell meant by that.

"We'd been married about two years when I found out he'd robbed a jewelry store at gunpoint and brutalized the owner, and that the police were looking for him. I'd had enough. I told him I was leaving him. He . . . he attacked me, savagely. He used a knife on me."

Viola flinched. "That little scar near your eyebrow . . ."

"That's the least of it. The rest are in places no one can see." Except for Will, who'd seen them for the first time that night before he left for France last month. *Stay*, she'd whispered as he'd lain in her bed, having come there to soothe her despair, and his, over his imminent departure for a war that might keep them apart for years, or even forever.

He hesitated, knowing, as Nell did, that this would be opening a door that could never be closed. But then he crushed her to him with trembling arms, and it was so painfully sweet, so fierce, so tender, so perfect, that the very memory of it made her heart quiver in her chest, her eyes sting hotly.

Bloody hell, he'd said as he lowered her night shift off her left shoulder, revealing the nine-inch scar that crawled in a pale ribbon from the outer edge of her collarbone down the side of her breast. Touching his lips to it, he'd whispered, *I wish to God I'd met you before he did. I wish . . . I wish . . .*

I know. Me, too.

"If you don't mind my saying so," Viola said, "Duncan *sounds* like a monster, having done that to you."

"And yet he also made a very noble sacrifice once that probably saved my life. But as grateful as I am for that, I can never forget what he took from me. You see, I was with child when Duncan . . . did that to me. I miscarried. It was an incomplete miscarriage, but I didn't realize that until I was reeling with fever from the infection. My landlady brought me to Dr. Greaves. He saved my life and took me in. I owe him a great deal."

Nell considered and swiftly rejected the notion of admitting to Viola the full extent of her relationship with Cyril Greaves. Gratitude had drawn her to his bed the first time, but after that it had been about other things—comfort, affection, their mutual loneliness. Although of different religions, they'd shared the same values, including a respect for the sanctity of marital vows—ironic, given that they were both married, albeit to spouses with whom they were unlikely to ever again cohabit. During the three years they'd slept together, Nell had refused, on religious grounds, to let him use a French letter, despite which she had never conceived. She'd taken this as proof—they both had—that she'd been rendered barren by the infection that had ravaged her after the miscarriage.

"I like Cyril," Viola said.

"He's a very likable man."

"Duncan was convicted and sent to prison, I take it?"

"For thirty years."

"I don't suppose you've considered divorce.

Even with the stigma, it strikes me as a more acceptable prospect than spending the rest of your life bound in wedlock to someone like that."

"When I was a practicing Catholic," Nell said, "it was a futile option. The only reason to divorce Duncan would have been to remarry, and if I'd done that, I would have been excommunicated."

"But now?" Viola said.

"I went to speak to Duncan last month. That was the purpose of my trip to the prison. I told him I wanted a divorce, and he flew into a rage. He says I'm all he's got, and that a marriage in the Church can never be undone. I ended up on the floor, with him on top of me screaming about how he was going to write to you and Mr. Hewitt and tell you about our marriage if I went forward with the divorce. I was afraid if he did that, Mr. Hewitt would insist on dismissing me even if you felt otherwise. In a choice between getting that divorce and losing Gracie . . . well, I had no choice."

"Right, well, it would appear that Mr. Skinner has beaten Duncan to the punch as regards the tell-all letter, and as you can see, your position with us is in no jeopardy."

"Only because you happened to see Skinner's

letter before Mr. Hewitt did. If Duncan writes, who's to say—"

"I shall make an effort to get to the mail before Mr. Hewitt does. It shouldn't be too difficult, even after we return to Boston—he's at India Wharf or the mill six days a week. So you see?" Viola spread her hands, smiling. "There's nothing to stop you petitioning for a divorce, if that's what you really want."

"It is," she said. "Desperately. I know it's a grueling and expensive process, but I'll do whatever I have to do. And I've saved a good deal of money over the years. I'm hopeful it will be enough to—"

"I'll pay for it," Viola said with a careless wave of her hand. "You shouldn't have to—"

"I'm paying for it, Mrs. Hewitt. It's a kind offer, but I think you've done enough for me, and I have quite a bit saved up, almost five thousand dollars."

With a startled little laugh, Viola said, "How on earth did you manage to put away that much?"

"Given that I don't have to pay for housing or food, it really wasn't very difficult. I'm not in the habit of spending money, so I just put it in the bank, instead, and let it earn interest. Do you think five thousand will cover the legal fees?"

"I should certainly hope so. As for it being a grueling process, you're right, it can take a very long time and a great deal of effort—or not. Do you recall my friend Libby Wentworth from church? She was granted her divorce decree within days of filing the petition."

"Within *days*?"

"It should come as no surprise to you that in the matter of divorce, as in so many other things, wealth and influence can go far toward smoothing the way. There are strings that can be pulled, corners that can be cut . . ."

"Money that can change hands?"

"Would you balk at that?"

"No." Nell had far too much at stake to indulge in such qualms.

Viola said, "Libby was represented by our mutual friend Silas Mead. Silas is one of the most powerful lawyers in Boston. They call him The Magician. I seem to recall that he and his wife have expressed an interest in this area of the Cape, what with it becoming such a fashionable summer destination now that one can get here by train. Why don't I invite them to spend this weekend with us? They can come down on the Friday train with August and Harry and Cecilia. I'll ask Silas to be prepared to meet with the two of us on a confidential legal matter."

"That would be wonderful," Nell said. "But if Mr. Hewitt were to find out why you invited them . . ."

"Silas is nothing if not discreet. If I ask him not to mention it to Mr. Hewitt, he won't. Meanwhile, I don't want you fretting about all this. You've lost your brother. That's enough of a burden. And I want you taking care of yourself. You've been looking so wan lately, and I know it's not just the heat. I think it's because you haven't been eating enough. I know you can't be trying to lose weight, a slender thing like you."

"Hardly. I just haven't had much of an appetite lately."

"That can happen in the summer."

Or in the initial weeks of pregnancy, thought Nell.

ELEVEN days, she mused as she washed off the bay water in the big bathroom down the hall from her third-floor bedroom. Eleven days since her monthly courses were due; it was the first time in the fourteen years she'd been getting them that they hadn't arrived with clockwork predictability. She'd been getting funny little twinges in her abdomen, too, and her breasts were oddly sensitive.

Laying her head back against the lip of the bathtub and closing her eyes, she cradled her lower belly with both hands, picturing the tiny, curled-up baby within—Will's baby, planted there on the eve of his departure for France. Nell had always longed for a child of her own, ever since she was very young. For the past ten years, she'd assumed she could never conceive. Had she thought it possible, she would have let Will "take measures to protect her," as he had suggested that night, such measures being less distasteful to her now that she was moving away from Catholicism.

On the one hand, this pregnancy was a godsend; on the other, a disaster. Once Nell started showing, she would be ruined. As sympathetic as Viola might be, the notion of a woman carrying an illegitimate child having the care of a young girl was unthinkable. A chambermaid like Annie McIntyre, who could be kept away from public view while her inconvenient pregnancy came to term, was one thing, a governess quite another. Mr. Hewitt and society at large would be outraged.

Nell's only hope, assuming she *could* secure a divorce, and quickly, was a hasty marriage. If Will were here, she had little doubt that he would offer to do the right thing. Even when he was at his lowest, with opium seething in his veins and a nihilistic disinterest in whether he lived or died, William Hewitt had always been a gentleman with a gentleman's instincts, especially as regarded women. Although, as Will's wife, Nell would no longer be Gracie's governess, she would be married to Gracie's father; Viola would be her mother-in-law. She would have as much access to the child as she liked. And she would have retained her precious, hard-won reputation.

It would remain to be seen, of course, how satisfying she would find such a marriage. Would Will stop gambling and roaming and settle down? *Could* he settle down?

Such speculation was, of course, purely academic, given that Will wasn't here. He was very far away and completely incommunicado, with no plans to return to Boston anytime soon. Even if the divorce came through, Nell was likely to end up ruined. It was a crushing dilemma, and one for which she had no solution.

Don't surrender to this, she counseled herself for

the hundredth time since realizing she was with child. *You can't help yourself—or your baby—if you let this situation overwhelm you.*

Nell finished her bath and dried off. As she was buttoning her dressing gown, her gaze lit on the miniature claw-foot tub where the Hewitt boys had been bathed when they were infants, and where Nell had bathed Gracie her initial summer here at Falconwood after she'd been appointed the child's governess. Nell had gasped with delight the first time she'd seen that darling little tub. Of all the luxurious trappings at Falconwood, it had been, and still was, her favorite. How excited little Gracie used to get when it was bath time; how she used to coo and splash and shriek with laughter. Nell used to imagine having her own baby, and a tub like that in which to bathe him.

And of course, a husband with whom to share him.

Nell touched her forehead, saying, *"In nomine Patris,"* before remembering that she was a Protestant now, more or less, and Protestants didn't make the sign of the cross.

She hesitated, then made it anyway, just for good measure. "Jesus, son of David, have pity on me," she whispered. "I may have sinned to get this baby, but don't punish him for that. Don't let him be fatherless. And don't let me lose Gracie, I beg you." She started to say "Amen" before realizing she wasn't quite done.

Summoning up the words she'd said over the bodies of her brothers and sisters, her mother, and far too many others over the years, she said, "Absolve, we beseech Thee, O Lord, the soul of thy servant James Murphy, whether he be my brother or not, that being dead to this world he may live to Thee, and whatever sins he may have committed in this life through human frailty, do Thou of Thy most merciful goodness forgive. Through our Lord Jesus Christ Thy Son who with Thee liveth and reigneth in the unity of the Holy Ghost, world without end. Amen."

Chapter 3

"**Y**OU'RE his sister?" asked Chief Constable Phineas Bryce skeptically.

"If you're wondering why I'm not in mourning," said Nell with a glance down at her pewter silk day dress, "I'm holding off on that until I'm sure that the James Murphy who died in that fire was, indeed, my brother."

"Actually," said the thickset, steely-haired constable, "I was wondering how a fella called Murphy could have a sister named Sweeney. It is *Miss* Sweeney, isn't it?"

Nell hadn't even thought about that. Dr. Greaves—*Cyril*—sitting next to Nell in front of the constable's big, paper-strewn desk, evidently had. "Miss Sweeney is Mr. Murphy's stepsister," he said. Nell was surprised that the principled Cyril Greaves could utter such a facile lie so smoothly.

"If it was a different James Murphy who died in that fire," Nell said, "I shall be on my way."

Chief Bryce got up and retrieved a small pasteboard box and a hefty volume from a bookcase. He opened the box and handed it across to Nell, saying, "These here are the personal effects salvaged from Murphy's remains by the coroner, Mr. Leatherby, before the autopsy Monday night—except for the key to the Cunningham house, which was in his pocket. That's how we know for sure he was one of the men that burgled the place and shot the wife."

Inside the box were a belt buckle, a gold coin, a fragment of handkerchief linen, a pocket knife, a tortoiseshell comb, and a pair of spectacles with cracked lenses, all scorched.

"Jamie doesn't wear eyeglasses," Nell said. The coin was a five-dollar piece, Nell thought, given its size and the eagle and shield imprinted on it. Finding it odd that a half eagle should be nestled in this box rather than in the pocket of one of Chief Bryce's "boys," Nell lifted it to examine more closely. It appeared to be made not of gold, but of brass, with the legend WAR OF 1861 along the upper edge, in which a hole had been punched.

"That's an identification tag," Cyril said. "Turn it over."

Nell did so, finding, in lieu of the liberty head she would have expected, a flat disk stamped with lettering.

JA^S MURPHY.
C^O. E.
9TH REG. INF.
MASS. VOL.
BOSTON.

Cyril said, "It was always a challenge, during the war, trying to identify the dead. If a soldier was getting ready to go into battle, he might buy one of these from the sutler who sold them their provisions, and wear it around his neck—just in case. Some veterans hold on to them as good luck tokens, or mementoes."

"He'd been wearing it on a string around his

neck," Bryce said. "Course, the string mostly burned away."

"I doubt very much that the man this belonged to was my brother," Nell said, returning it to the box. "Jamie isn't the type to have enlisted."

"Even with all the patriotic fervor at the time?" Cyril asked.

"It wouldn't have affected him," she said. "He's irresponsible, devil may care."

"How old was he the last time you saw him, Nell?"

"Fifteen."

"Well, then, isn't it possible he—"

"You didn't know him," she said. "He was such . . . such a child. A real charmer, but he never cared about anything except getting something for nothing. Getting money without working for it, getting girls to . . ." She glanced at Chief Bryce, thumbing through the big leather-bound volume. "Grant him their favors without offering so much as a pair of glass ear bobs."

"This should settle it," said Chief Bryce as he leafed through the book, with its thick, strangely stiff pages. "This here's our 'Rogues' Gallery.' It's pictures of the hard tickets we've put away these past few years, the worst of the lot, anyway. Some of them we just tore out of the *Police Gazette*, but we've got a fella in town that owns a photograph parlor, and we pay him to make photographs of the bad pennies, the ones we keep arresting over and over. James Murphy was one of them."

He thumped the open book down on the desk facing Nell and Cyril. The page on the right was inked with handwritten notes. That on the left was a folio with an oval cutout bordered in gold that served to frame a photograph of a blond, bespectacled young man in a rumpled jacket and limp bow tie.

Nell heard a despairing moan as the air rushed from her lungs. She sat forward for a better view of the photograph, which had a slightly washed-out look to it except for the eyes, those crystalline eyes that had always managed to look both guileless and devilish at the same time. "No," she whispered.

"That's not him?" Bryce said.

"No, I think it is," Cyril said quietly.

Nell tried to pull the book toward her in order to see it better, but it was heavy. Cyril lifted it and held it at an angle over her lap. Scrawled in a bottom corner of the photograph was *Mar. '69*, which was more than ten years after the last time Nell had seen him. Jamie's boyish face had grown sinewy; whiskers glinted on his jaw. His right eyebrow was bisected by a faint scar coursing diagonally across his forehead, disappearing into a shock of unkempt cornsilk hair.

Nell whispered his name, shaking her head. "I thought . . . I thought it couldn't be him. I didn't want it to be him."

"I know," Cyril said. "I'm sorry, Nell."

The notes on the right-hand page were written in several different hands:

James Killian Murphy

b. Feb. 12, 1844 ~ Murphy is five feet 11 inches tall, slim built, fair hair, blond complexion, blue eyes, clean-shaven with short side whiskers, high forehead with knife scar. Wears spectacles. May seek employment as laborer or dockhand.

Sept. 15, 1859, robbed livery driver Julius Finch of a pouch of banknotes belonging to Falmouth Nat'l Bank. Sentenced Nov. '59 to 18 months hard labor, Plymth. Hse. of Corr.

Dec. 4, 1864, robbed Yarmouth-Woods Hole stage

*with accomplice David Quinn, both sentenced to 3
years hard labor, Plymouth House of Corrections.*

*Mar. 27, 1869, attmpt'd theft of ladies reticule from
coat hook in Babbitt's Choc. Shop, East Falmth, sent.
in May of that yr. to 8 mo's Plymth. Hse. of Corr.*

*July 19, 1870, with accomplice murdered Susannah
Cunningham of Boston, aged 37 yrs., in course of
armed burglary at Cunningham summer home at 175
Grand Ave., Falmouth Heights. Burned to death while
a fugitive from justice July 31, 1870, aged 26 yrs.*

Nell reread the last entry with a kind of woozy
horror. *Murdered Susannah Cunningham of Boston,
aged 37 yrs. . . . Burned to death . . .*

"This accomplice is still in hiding?" she asked
the constable.

Bryce nodded. "Davey Quinn, that's who we think
it is, on account of him and Murphy been pulling
holdups together for years, and I've never known either one of them to team up with anybody else. My
boys have been putting up placards with Quinn's picture on them, and we've had some nibbles that make
us think he might still be on the Cape—which is the
last place he should be, seeing as he's a wanted man
here, but you'd be surprised, some of the dumb

things some of these pugs do. Quinn, he's not only dumb, he's a hothead. Your brother was the voice of reason in that particular partnership, and the brains, too—but even he stayed on the Cape. There's no accounting, but then, who knows the way their minds work, these gutter prowlers."

"Which one actually shot Mrs. Cunningham?" Nell asked. "My brother or this Davey Quinn?"

"We don't know, but it's not really important. Under the law, if somebody gets killed during the course of a crime, all the hoods involved are guilty of felony murder, and they'll all hang. It doesn't matter who actually pulled the trigger."

It mattered to Nell. It mattered very greatly. She said, "I'm afraid I know very little about this crime, Constable. Can you tell me about it?"

Sitting back in his chair, Bryce laced his fingers over his burly chest. "It happened Tuesday, July nineteenth, around dawn. The cook was the only one awake at that hour, 'cause she had to start the coffee and whatnot. So, she's in her room on the second floor of the carriage house, getting dressed—that's where the servants bunk, the carriage house—and she hears a scream from the main house that she knows has to be Mrs. Cunningham, on account of she was the only one who'd slept there that night."

"Her husband wasn't there?" asked Cyril. "Does he just come down from Boston on weekends?"

"Nah, he's been there the whole summer, along with the wife. He likes to sail—got a forty-foot sloop he's real proud of. He calls it the *Oh, Susannah*, after his wife. It's his pride and joy, and the envy of all his neighbors in Falmouth Heights. But he'd gotten called away to New York on business— he's in shipping. He'd left the day before, and he was due back at the end of the week. And they didn't have any kids, so it was just the missus in the house."

Cyril said, "I'm surprised he left her there all alone while he was gone."

"He didn't mean to," Bryce said. "She was supposed to spend that week at her sister's place on Martha's Vineyard, but a bad storm blew in over Vineyard Sound that afternoon, and they had to cancel the ferry."

"So the cook heard a scream," Nell said.

"Closely followed by a gunshot. She looked out the window and saw two men run out of the house and drive off in a wagon that was parked out back, but it wasn't light enough yet for her to make out their faces. She woke up the driver and the butler, and the three of them went into the house and found Mrs. Cunningham laying there in the entrance to the library with a bullet hole smack in the middle of her forehead and the carpet soaked with blood. They sent for us, and me and a couple of the boys had a look around. From what we could tell, the only thing that had been disturbed was one of those display cabinets, a big one, about five feet square and two feet deep, made out of mahogany and plate glass. Inside, there's this whole collection of antique nautical instruments—sextants, quadrants, chronometers, compasses . . . There's even a three-hundred-year-old, what do you call it, aster, astro . . ."

"Astrolabe?" Cyril said.

"Yeah, it's the jewel of the collection, according to Cunningham—the husband, Frederick Cunningham. We cabled him with the news about his wife, and he came back that day. He was sobbing when he got off the train at the Falmouth depot, and he didn't stop till we'd poured about a pint of brandy into him. When he'd calmed down enough to talk, he told us about the collection. He said the astrolabe had been on Magellan's ship when he went around the world."

"My God," said Cyril. "It must be worth thousands."

"Many tens of thousands, Cunningham said. He said the collection as a whole had been appraised at close to six figures. His wife's great-grandfather had put it together, and she had a strong sentimental attachment to it. He says it had been against the east wall of the library, but when we got there, it was near the door that let out onto the back porch. Those fellas—your brother and Quinn—were obviously trying to drag it outside so they could put it in their wagon. It would have taken them a while to get it as far as they did, 'cause it was heavy, with all those brass instruments inside. That's how we knew Murphy must have had a partner. Me and the boys could barely budge the damned—'scuse me, miss. We could barely move it."

"Then why do you suppose they didn't just open up the case and take the instruments out?" Nell asked.

"That's what I asked Cunningham," Bryce said. "He said the instruments were bolted to the shelves, and that the case was sealed shut to make it airtight. I asked him if there was anybody with a grudge against him who might have a key to the house, 'cause there was no sign of forced entry. He said he didn't have any enemies, and there were only three keys to the house—one for him, one for the missus, and a spare that he kept under a sundial in the garden. Only, when he went to look for it, it was gone. Somebody'd pinched it. Come to find out your brother had been doing yard work for the Cunninghams for a couple of weeks before the burglary, but of course we didn't make that connection till a couple of days ago, when we identified the burned body and asked Cunningham if the name 'James Murphy' rang a bell."

Of course? Had Nell been in charge of investigating this case, her first move would have been to question Mr. Cunningham as to who might have had access to their property.

"Obviously," said the constable, "your brother figured out that the stuff in that case was valuable, so he stole the key—which he stumbled across while he was working in the yard—so he could slip into the house and make off with it. He would have brung Quinn along just to help him move the thing, and he would have chosen a time when he thought nobody was home—not knowing that the wife had had to cancel her trip to Martha's Vineyard because of the weather. They wouldn't have made too much of an effort to keep quiet, thinking they were in an empty house. The carriage house is pretty far away. But then Mrs. C. hears a noise and comes downstairs, one of them pops her, and they flee the scene. They split up and went into hiding. Your brother found the cranberry shed at the Gilmartin farm, or maybe he already knew it was there, and that's where he decided to hole up."

"Was he there the whole time he was in hiding, do you know?" Nell asked.

"He would have to have been there for at least a week, 'cause one of the boarders told me—"

"Boarders?" Nell said.

Bryce said, "Yeah, Mrs. Gilmartin rents out rooms 'cause the cranberries aren't enough to support them, but she's got this great big farmhouse for just her and her daughter. This boarder, fella named George, told me things had gone missing from the house the Sunday before. They'd been at Mass, the mother, the daughter, and all the boarders. There was an ice cream social afterward, so they all stayed in town but the daughter, who went back home to get a lamb stew started for supper."

"Doesn't seem quite fair," Cyril said, "making her miss out on the festivities."

"George said she offered, on account of she had a stomach gripe, so she didn't want any ice cream. When they came home later, she told them she'd found some of the shortbread gone that her ma had made that morning to go with the stew, and some blueberries. There was some ham loaf missing from the ice closet, and a meat knife from a hook on the wall. A quart of milk, too. They started looking around and found an old quilt and a blanket and a pillow gone from the beds. There was some other stuff, I think. I can't remember it all."

Because you didn't bother to write it down. "Then, a week later," Nell said, "the cranberry shed caught fire."

"Any idea what started it?" Cyril asked.

"Maybe he fell asleep with a cigarette in his hand," suggested the constable with a negligent shrug.

"Jamie didn't smoke," Nell said.

"Not when you knew him," Cyril said, "but perhaps—"

"And there's no match safe in there," she said, nodding toward the pasteboard box.

"A candle fell over, then," Bryce said. "Or a lantern. The shed goes up in flames, the daughter raises the alarm . . ."

"After getting trapped in the fire herself," Cyril interjected.

"What?" Bryce said. "What are you talking about?"

"I treated her for smoke inhalation yesterday morning," said Cyril. "She just barely made it out of that shed alive."

"Didn't she tell you?" Nell asked.

"She wasn't around when I was called over there the next morning," the constable said. "I think the mother said she was up in her room. I never even seen her."

Nor, obviously, did he seek her out.

"Did she mention what she was doing in the shed when you treated her yesterday?" Nell asked Cyril.

He hesitated, looking grim. "She said she'd heard a man screaming for help."

Nell sat back, her eyes shut, very sorry she'd asked.

Cyril rested a hand on her shoulder. Quietly he said, "Don't think about it, Nell. Don't torment yourself."

"In any event," the constable continued, "the shed burned down. Well, not completely. They managed to get the fire put out, thanks to the boarders.

They formed a bucket brigade from Mill Pond to the cranberry shed. Got it put out pretty quick, so the shed's still standing, but there's not much left of it. I came out with a couple of fellas from Packer's Mortuary here in town, to look things over and get the body out of there. It was in better shape than I expected 'cause of how quick they got the fire put out—charred and all, but just on the front," he said, patting his chest, "'cause he'd been laying on his back on a folded-up quilt."

Don't think about it.

"Constable," Cyril said, "must you be so graphic? Miss Sweeney *is* his sister, after all, and—"

"It's all right, Cyril," Nell said. She would rather Bryce spoke frankly than to pick and choose what he told them.

Bryce said, "Leatherby, the coroner, ordered an autopsy, which is required in cases of accidental death, so a local surgeon did it that night."

"Which surgeon?" Cyril asked.

"Dr. Monk. You know him?"

"I know all the doctors on the Cape." A vague answer, no doubt deliberately so. As Nell recalled, Cyril had little respect for the abilities of Chauncey Monk, who'd gotten his training through wartime apprenticeship rather than medical school. "Did the autopsy turn up anything significant?"

"Nah, he died from the fire."

"The fire or the smoke?" Nell asked, hoping it was the latter.

"Monk didn't say."

And you didn't ask. How very unsurprising.

"I don't suppose you get too many murder cases in this neck of the woods," Nell said.

"This would be my first," Bryce replied. "There hasn't been anybody hanged on the Cape in fifty years."

"Is my brother's body still in the mortuary?" she asked, hoping he hadn't been buried in some paupers' cemetery.

Chief Bryce looked down, scratching his chin. "Yeah, it's, uh, it's still there, but—"

"Well, that's something." Turning to Cyril, Nell said, "If you don't mind, I'd like to visit the mortuary after we leave here, and then St. Catherine's in East Falmouth, so that I can see to his final arrangements."

"That should make Claire Gilmartin happy," said Cyril. "While I was examining her yesterday, she seemed very concerned that he be buried in consecrated ground. She's extremely pious, and a bit . . . not simple, but quite naive. She said it wouldn't be right to deny him a proper burial with a priest officiating just because he was a criminal, that God loves sinners just as much as He loves the rest of us."

"How did she know he was Catholic?" Nell asked.

"Murphy?" he said. "It would be *my* guess."

Chief Bryce, who'd been following this exchange with an oddly strained expression, said, "I, uh, I don't think you're gonna be able to have him buried."

"But I'm his next of kin," Nell said.

"Yeah, but see, the body's already been sold."

"Sold?"

"I should have known," muttered Cyril.

"It's been embalmed and sold to Harvard Medical School to be anatomized," Bryce said. "It's being shipped up to Boston next—"

"My brother's body is not going anywhere," Nell said slowly, her voice quivering ever so slightly as she strove to contain her fury, "except to St. Catherine's to be buried in the churchyard next to my mother and the rest of my brothers and sisters. God help you or anyone else who tries to prevent that."

"Hey, it was Packer and Monk that arranged for the sale," Bryce said. "Talk to them."

"Wait a minute," said Cyril. "You can't dissect a body that's been autopsied. Well, you can, but it wouldn't be much good for teaching purposes, with all the organs removed."

"I understand Dr. Monk made an effort to disturb the remains as little as possible for that reason," Bryce said.

"Did they even try to find out whether my brother had any family?" Nell demanded heatedly. "Or did they just—"

"It's all right, Nell," said Cyril, patting her back. "We'll go to Packer's and—"

"Get off of me!" yelled a man from somewhere on the other side of the constable's office door. "It'd be 'interference' if you bastards knew what you were doing, but you're a bunch of blundering incompetents, every last man among you."

Chief Bryce pulled a face. "That's the husband, Fred Cunningham. He's in here every day, sometimes twice a day, checking up on us, seeing if we've got any new leads, telling us how to do our jobs . . . The rest of the time, he's out there snooping around and making a pest of himself. Hey, I sympathize with him. He's a grieving husband, he wants justice for his wife. But I wish he'd just trust us to—"

A knock came at the door, which squeaked open to reveal a ginger-haired young constable holding out a handbill. "Sorry to interrupt you, Chief, but he's at it again. Klingmann found him passing these out in Davey Quinn's neighborhood."

Bryce took the handbill, grimacing as he read it. "This is even worse than the last one. Next, he'll be asking for the guy's head on a spike."

Nell looked through the open doorway to see a fortyish man with wild, red-rimmed eyes trying to muscle his way between two big men blocking Chief Bryce's door. "That includes you, Bryce!" he screamed, stabbing a finger in the chief's direction. "All you do is tack up posters and sit around waiting for tips that never come, and you get mad when I go out and actually look for the son of a bitch. What do you think, if you wait long enough, he's just going to just walk in here and give himself up?"

"Tell him I'll be out there to listen to his current rant just as soon as I'm finished up here," Bryce instructed the young constable, who backed up and closed the door.

"May I?" asked Nell as she reached for the handbill.

With a *why not* look, Bryce handed over the bill. Nell held it so that Cyril could read it, too.

$3,000 REWARD!!!

FOR THE CAPTURE OF **DAVID QUINN**, WANTED FOR

M U R D E R !

TURN HIM IN DEAD

Or Alive

The sum of **THREE THOUSAND DOLLARS** is offered by Mr. Frederick Cunningham of Falmouth Heights and Boston, Mass., upon presentation of the **BODY** or person of **DAVID QUINN**. As **DAVID QUINN** is known to be a first-rate marksman who is furthermore possessed of an excitable temperament, any attempt to capture him alive should be undertaken only by armed lawmen. Others are encouraged to employ whatever means necessary to subdue **DAVID QUINN** before he can vent his murderous rage.

An additional award of **TWO THOUSAND DOLLARS** will be paid upon receipt of the **CORPSE** of **DAVID QUINN** within three months from the date of this circular, provided it is delivered in recognizable condition.

DESCRIPTION.

DAVID QUINN is 29 years old; 5 feet 7 inches high; thinly built; hair dark and thin; complexion pale; eyes protruding somewhat; a moustache of dark color; teeth defective; speaks rather quickly from the nose, in a high tone of voice; has a brisk gait; manner jerky and erratic; wears a bowler hat.

IF KILLED or captured, address all information, telegraphic or otherwise, to **FREDERICK E. CUNNINGHAM** at either of these addresses:

175 Grand Avenue, Falmouth Heights, Mass.,

64 Beacon Street, Boston, Mass.

August 3rd, 1870

Bryce said, "Obviously Cunningham wants the bas—Davey Quinn not just arrested, but stone-cold dead. I can't say as I'd feel any different if it was my wife that took a bullet to the brain, but by circulating something like that in Davey Quinn's neighborhood, he's basically soliciting murder. A worse assortment of ruffians and plug-uglies you can't imagine."

Unfortunately, Nell could imagine them all too well, having lived among that breed for two years. Animals like that would knife their own mothers in the back for a bottle of rum.

Bryce said, "Cunningham accuses us of not putting enough effort into the case, but when he had the chance to help us—*really* help us, not just play vigilante—he refused. When he first came back from New York, I asked if he wouldn't mind posting a reward for information leading to the identification and arrest of his wife's killers, say a thousand bucks, but he turned me down. Said he didn't have that kind of money, on account of his business had started foundering, said the bank was threatening to foreclose on both his beach house and his home in Boston."

"Then how can he offer three thousand dollars for Quinn's capture?" Cyril asked.

"It's five thousand if they kill him, which is really what he's looking for," Bryce said. "Even one of the dumb bashers this handbill is aimed at can read between the lines, but the way it's worded, Cunningham can claim that's not really what he means. The first batch of these bills showed up the very day after Murphy's body was identified, 'cause I'd made the mistake of telling Cunningham that we'd be looking for Quinn now. So two weeks after he turns me down for the thousand, he's offering five times that much to whoever kills Quinn. When I asked him where the money came from, he said he sold that case of nautical instruments to Cornelius Vanderbilt. He said it was enough money to dig him out of his hole, and then some."

"I thought that collection had sentimental value," Nell said.

"To the wife, not to him. In fact, he told me he loathed the sight of it, 'cause it was the reason his wife got killed, said he couldn't wait to get it out of the house."

"I'D like to see my brother," Nell told Mr. Packer after he finally agreed, with a churlish lack of grace, to cancel the sale of Jamie's body and prepare him for burial in a fine walnut coffin, wearing a proper suit of clothes.

"Right this way," said the officious little toad as he ushered her and Cyril downstairs to a cryptlike basement redolent of death and carbolic.

"Nell, are you sure you want to do this?" asked Cyril as Mr. Packer opened a door into what he called the "Cold Room" and stood waiting for them to enter. "It's bound to be a very unpleasant sight."

"I've seen dead bodies before, if you recall. You should also recall that I have a fairly strong stomach."

"This is your brother, Nell, and people who've died this way . . ." He closed his hands over her shoulders and said, "If you see him like this, this is how you'll remember him. You won't be able to help it."

Nell wanted to argue with him—this was her only chance, after all, to view her last remaining family member before his body was committed to the earth—but she had to grudgingly admit that he was right about remembering. If only she could forget the sight of her mother's desiccated face frozen in a grimace of agony after the bout of Asiatic cholera that wrung the life out of her within the space of a single day.

"Let me go in first," said Cyril. "And then if it's . . . not too bad . . ."

Nell nodded at the floor.

She sat on a little hard-backed chair at the bottom of the stairs listening to the hiss of the gas jets until he emerged from the room about five minutes later. Softly he said, "Jamie wouldn't want you to see him like that."

Neither of them spoke as he escorted her out to the sunlit street and handed her up into his coupé. He settled next to her and unwrapped the reins from the brake handle, but then he just sat there, gazing down the road in a preoccupied way.

"Cyril?"

"I lost Charlotte," he said without looking at her.

Nell stared at him as it sank in. "She . . . ?"

"About a year and a half ago. It was cancer, but it was quick, thank God. They had to keep her in the psychiatric wing because . . . well, she'd become so delusional that they couldn't handle her on a regular floor. But they kept her comfortable."

"Cyril." Touching his arm, Nell said, "I'm so sorry. I had no idea." She wondered why he hadn't told her this yesterday, but it was a question she kept to herself.

He flicked the reins; the buggy rattled over the

brick road. "If it's any comfort to you, Nell, I think I can say with some measure of confidence that your brother succumbed to smoke inhalation rather than to the fire itself."

A bit thrown by the abrupt conversational shift, but heartened by this news, Nell said, "How did you conclude that?"

"You may find the details a bit—"

"Would you *please* stop trying to protect me and just tell me?" In a milder tone of voice, she added another "Please."

After a moment's hesitation, he said, "The flesh *is* charred, more so on the trunk and limbs than the head, I assume because his clothing caught fire. But as Chief Bryce mentioned, the entire dorsal aspect is relatively unscathed—skin, hair, clothing . . . There are even some bits of a wool blanket that must have been tucked around him. It's clear that he was lying flat on his back, unmoving, when the flames reached him, and that could only have been the case if he'd been dead or unconscious."

She said, "Thank you, Cyril. It does comfort me to know that."

"There's a Y incision on the torso, and several others from the embalming, but the head was untouched. Mustn't disturb such valuable remains, eh?"

"I haven't seen you in church this summer," said genial old Father Donnelly as he gestured Nell into an armchair in his book-lined office; Cyril, not wanting to intrude, was giving himself a tour of the modest little stone church.

"Um . . ."

Lowering his considerable bulk into the chair opposite Nell's, he said, in his timeworn brogue, "Don't tell me those Boston Brahmins have gone and turned my pious little Nell Sweeney into a Protestant. Port?" he asked, lifting a decanter from the table next to him.

Relieved that he didn't seem to expect a response to the "Protestant" comment, she declined the port and said, "Father, did you happen to see yesterday's extra to the *Barnstable Patriot*?"

The priest shook his head mournfully as he poured his glass of port. "If you're asking whether I heard about Jamie, the answer is yes. I can't tell you how it grieved me. I'm that sorry. A terrible thing. Terrible. Terrible."

"I'm surprised you even remember Jamie," Nell said. "He hasn't attended Mass here since he was a child." As an adolescent, he'd always balked at going to church, even at Christmas and Easter.

"Oh, sure, he used to show up every once in a while when he wasn't behind bars, 'specially the past few years. Late Mass, usually. I suppose that would be why you never ran into him during your summers here. You were always partial to the early Mass."

The realization that she and Jamie had come so close to crossing paths was deeply saddening to Nell. "I've come here to arrange for his funeral Mass, Father, and for him to be buried in the churchyard alongside Ma and Tess and the rest of them."

Father Donnelly lowered his glass to the table slowly, frowning in a troubled way. He started to say something, then looked away, murmuring, "Oh, dear, dear, dear."

"What's wrong?" Nell asked. "Is it because he was a criminal? I know he lived a life of sin, but given how he grew up, is it any wonder?"

"Aye, but *you* didn't turn to sin," the priest said.

Nell gave him a look that said, *Oh, didn't I?* Father Donnelly had been her confessor when she was regarded in low-life circles as the most deft pick-pocket on the Cape.

He chuckled, ducking his head as if to concede her point. No matter how grim the circumstances, Father Donnelly never lost his good humor; it was one of the reasons his parishioners found him so engaging and easy to open up to.

Nell said, "You're always talking about God's mercy, Father, about how He loves us all, even the sinners. If that's so, then Jamie is as deserving of a church funeral as any of us."

Taking a sip of port, the priest said, "Between you and Claire Gilmartin, I've been subjected to quite the theological harangue these past couple of days."

"Claire Gilmartin? She's one of your parishioners?"

"Sure, and she lives just down the road on Mill Pond. She's here every Sunday with her mother, Hannah, and her boarders. Mrs. Gilmartin insists they attend Mass, or they can't live at her house. A harder worker you never saw. With all she's got on her hands, managing the farm and the boarding-house, she still finds time to come here and weed my flower garden, or bring me some eggs from her hens, or fruit from her trees, or a cake she baked, that kind of thing. I know you'd recognize her and Claire if you saw them. Claire, she's a sweet girl, too sweet for her own good, I sometimes think. But you should have heard her light into me about burying your brother in the churchyard."

"Does the Church actually *forbid* certain people from being buried in consecrated ground, or is it more a matter of . . . tradition?"

"Oh, no, canon law expressly denies Christian burial to heretics, excommunicants, the unbaptized, those who've died in a duel or who've taken a life, including their own, those who hold the Sacraments in contempt . . . Actually, all notorious sinners who die without repentance are excluded."

"How do you know for sure Jamie wasn't repentant?"

"Well . . ."

"I know priests sometimes bend the rules, Father. I know *you* have."

"God save me from you headstrong Irish lasses," he chuckled.

"Bury him in the churchyard, Father," Nell implored, her hands clasped as if in prayer. "Bury him with his mother and his brothers and sisters. If God really is as merciful as you've always told me, it would be the right thing to do, the only thing to do."

Father Donnelly studied her for a long moment, and then he drained his glass of port. "So, have you turned Protestant on me, or not?"

Her hesitation must have been telling, because he poured himself another port and tossed that one back as well. "Jesus, Mary, and Joseph," he said, but there was a glint of amusement in his eye when he said, "Who would have ever thought I'd be knuckling under to a Protestant?"

Chapter 4

"Y OU'RE not having dessert, Nell?" Viola asked Friday evening as her dinner to celebrate Harry and Cecilia's return from their honeymoon was drawing to a close. "You've always loved Mrs. Waters's coconut cake."

"It's the heat," Nell said, although it was, in fact, a pleasantly cool evening. "I don't have much of an appetite in the summer."

"I'm sure you're exhausted, too," said Cyril, seated opposite her at the long, damask-draped dining table. "It's been a rather trying day for you."

Jamie had been buried that morning in St. Catherine's churchyard following a funeral Mass celebrated by Father Donnelly and attended by Nell, Cyril, and a handful of Jamie's acquaintances, mostly young females who wept uncontrollably. Not so Nell, who had yet to shed a tear over her brother's demise. She wanted to weep, she wanted to scream and rail, but it all felt vaguely unreal.

Upon their return to Falconwood, they found that the newlywed couple, the Meads, and August Hewitt had just arrived in four hackney coaches from the Falmouth train depot. Harry's valet and Cecilia's lady's maid, personal laundress, and hairdresser had traveled in one of the hacks; her luggage for the four-day visit occupied another.

Cecilia's costume for this evening's dinner, a confection of blue and gold silk taffeta, was one of four dozen gowns created for her by the House of Worth during the Paris leg of her honeymoon. The plunging, pearl-encrusted bodice gripped her handspan waist; the skirt, an engineering marvel of swags, ruffles, and ruching, was fashionably narrow in front, the bulk of it having been hauled up in back to form a mountainous bustle and a train that would have done the Empress Eugenie proud. Complementing the regal effect were the diamond combs tucked into the mass of blond curls atop her head. More diamonds dangled from her ears and encircled her throat, along with Harry's wedding gift to her, a rope of pearls two yards long.

To Cecilia, who'd spent the better part of the afternoon being bathed and groomed, Nell's modest, long-sleeved gown—dyed black yesterday, along with the rest of her wardrobe—was nothing less than pitiable; Nell could see it in her eyes. *Oh, you poor thing,* she'd exclaimed when Nell told her that she was in mourning for her brother. *Black is so dreary, and so terribly unflattering. You must be in absolute despair.*

"I must say, the Cape is a good deal more civilized than I had been led to believe," said Silas Mead's wife, an auburn-haired beauty named Althea, who looked to be a good deal younger than he. "I'd expected something wild and desolate, but it's really quite beautiful—this area, at least."

"I'm told Falmouth Heights is where the better sort are summering now," Cecilia said. "They say there are grand houses and hotels going up every day."

"Too true," came a sotto voce grumble from the head of the table. The patrician, silver-haired August Hewitt, who'd built this house here twenty-five years ago precisely because Cape Cod *wasn't* a fashionable summer destination overrun with Bostonians and New Yorkers, made no secret of his dismay over its sudden popularity.

"Perhaps *we* could build a house in Falmouth Heights," Cecilia suggested to her new husband.

"I thought you wanted Newport," Harry mumbled into his seventh glass of wine before draining it and holding it up for refill. Matrimony appeared to suit Cecilia better than Harry, judging from his omnipresent aura of resigned misery. Although as dashingly turned out as always—he sported a gold brocade vest with his white tie and tails—the "Beau Brummel of Boston" looked a good decade older than when he'd set out on his honeymoon four months ago with his glittering bride, her servants, and her myriad trunks and hatboxes. His eyes were dead and his skin sallow, pointing up the scar on his left eyelid and the bulge on the bridge of his nose, permanent reminders of his unsuccessful, absinthe-stoked attempt two years ago to force himself on Nell.

"We can build a house in Falmouth Heights and another in Newport," Cecilia said. "Why not?"

"Yes, why not?" Harry drawled thickly. "What's another hundred grand here or there?"

"Oh, don't be such a grouch-pot." Forming her rosebud lips into an exaggerated pout, she pitched her voice childishly high and said, "*Please*, Harry? Pretty please? Pretty, pretty, pretty—"

"Fine," he growled. "Whatever you want. I can't imagine what I was thinking, questioning your wishes."

She let out a shrieking giggle of delight that made the glassware on the table quiver ever so slightly. Harry closed his eyes, a muscle in his jaw twitching. Imagining the decades of marital desolation stretching out before him, Nell almost felt sorry for him.

Almost.

"It *is* beautiful here, extraordinarily so," said Mr. Mead in an apparent attempt to redirect the conversation to its former subject. Though he looked to be in his sixties, and was almost entirely bald, the renowned lawyer exuded an aura of vigor and intellect that Nell couldn't help but find attractive; no wonder he had such a pretty young wife. "I say, Hewitt, it's a shame you can only get down here on weekends."

"I was here for the entire first week," said Mr. Hewitt as he scooped up a forkful of cake, "and when I come back here next weekend, I shall remain until the end of August. In the meantime, however, my business concerns must come first. The Tremont Street house is closed up, of course. I bunk with the Thorpes during the week."

"Ah, Leo. Capital fellow. Say, I'd love to take one of those shells out tomorrow. What say you, Hewitt? Care to race me across the bay?"

"Good Lord, no. It's been years since I've gotten into one of those things. The rheumatism, you know."

"What about you, Martin?" Mead asked. "I know *you* won't turn me down."

"I hate to," said the Hewitts' fair-haired youngest son, "but I've got to go back to Boston tomorrow so that I can preach at King's Chapel Sunday."

"Oh yes, I heard you'd been ordained. Congratulations, son."

"Thank you, sir."

August Hewitt, a devout Congregationalist who had vigorously opposed Martin's ordination as a Unitarian minister, glowered at the centerpiece of roses and candles.

Cradling her coffee cup as she lounged back in her chair, Althea Mead said, "Where do you live now, Martin? With the family house closed up, I assume you've gotten your own digs."

"I've been staying at Will's house on Acorn Street while I look for a place of my own. He gave me the key before he went overseas."

Mr. Hewitt gestured for another glass of whiskey, prompting a fretful look from his wife. On those rare occasions when he indulged in more than his usual one or two glasses of wine, he tended toward belligerence.

"Oh, lucky Will," said Cecilia, "going on holiday. Is he going to Paris? That's my very favorite city in the world. We spent most of April there. I bought the most beautiful, beautiful things. Harry, why don't we go back next month? We can buy one of those lovely townhouses with wrought iron balconies so that when we visit there, we don't have to stay in—"

"France is at war now, remember?" Harry said wearily. "Against Prussia?"

Cecilia pulled a face. "I *hate* wars. I hope it's over soon. Nell, if it's over before you marry Dr. Hewitt, perhaps he'll take you to Paris on *your* honeymoon."

Cyril lowered his fork and stared at Nell.

Oh, hell.

When people ask about our presumed engagement, Will had counseled in his farewell letter, *simply*

*tell them that you ended it over my gambling, aim-
lessness, and various other bad habits and defects of
character; no one will question that.*

Avoiding Cyril's eyes, Nell said, "We, um . . .
Dr. Hewitt and I have ended our engagement by
mutual agreement."

"What?" Cecilia gasped. *"Why?"*

Harry snorted at the tactless question. Mr. Hewitt
swallowed his brandy with a look of disgust, perhaps
because of Cecilia's rudeness, or perhaps because he
simply loathed the very mention of Will's name.

Nell said, "Um . . . well . . ."

Viola came to her rescue. "My eldest son travels
a great deal, and it appears to be a difficult habit to
break. He and Nell have decided, quite amicably,
that it would put too much of a strain upon their
marriage for him to be home so infrequently."

"Where does he travel to?" Cecilia asked.

"Wherever there are gaming hells and opium
dens," Mr. Hewitt muttered under his breath.

Those at the farthest end of the table might not
have heard him, but Cyril, who was sitting fairly
close, clearly did. He met Nell's gaze soberly, then
lifted his coffee cup and took a sip.

Martin evidently heard, too. Looking from his

father to Cecilia, he said, "Actually, Will went to France at the request of President Grant to serve as a battle surgeon for Napoleon's army."

Mrs. Mead said, "The president himself requested him?"

"My brother was regarded as the finest battle surgeon in the Union Army."

"That's quite impressive," said Mr. Mead.

With another glance at his father, Martin said, "Yes, isn't it?"

"I won't lie to you," Silas Mead told Nell and Viola as he swirled his cognac in its snifter. "Massachusetts has some of the strictest divorce statutes in the country. The courts of the Commonwealth only grant about three hundred divorces a year. That's where I come in."

From the parlor across the house, where the others had retired for postprandial liqueurs, chess, and conversation, came muffled piano music that sounded almost atonal until Nell recognized it as an appallingly heavy-handed rendition of her favorite piece, Beethoven's "Moonlight" Sonata.

Cocking his head to listen, Mr. Mead said, "I know

that's not Althea. She plays with a rather more . . .
delicate touch."

"Silas, you are a born diplomatist," said Viola
with a little chuckle. "That's Cecilia, and she fan-
cies herself quite the pianist. I fear I shall have to
invent a rather creative repertoire of excuses to disappear after dinner while they're here."

Her excuse tonight was a desire to show Mr. Mead
the artwork she and Nell had executed that summer—
just a ruse, of course, for a private legal consultation
about Nell's marital situation, cooked up in advance
between the three of them. Grabbing the candelabra
off the dining table, she'd asked Nell to steer her
wheelchair to the domed greenhouse off the kitchen,
which she'd long ago pressed into service as a studio.
After a cursory tour of the paintings propped on
easels and tucked into drying racks, the lawyer and
Nell pulled up chairs and they got down to business.

"I've brought some papers for you to sign," Mr.
Mead told Nell. "I'll file them next week and follow
up on them aggressively, but you should know that
this process, even if successful, can be extremely
time-consuming. There are two facilitating factors
that can speed things along and help to ensure a fa-
vorable outcome. First, it would be helpful if you

could convince your husband not to contest the divorce."

"I don't think that will be possible," Nell said. "He's adamant that we remain married."

Viola said, "Does he understand—really understand—that you have no intention of living with him again as his wife, even after he's released from prison?"

"I've made that abundantly clear," Nell said. "He says he objects to the idea of divorce on religious grounds, because the Church doesn't recognize it, but really it's because he just can't let me go. When we were married, he became extremely possessive and jealous, with no reason to be. He tried to dictate what I could do and who I could talk to. I think he still wants that kind of control over me."

"If you can think of any argument that might sway him," said Mr. Mead, "now would be the time to make it. I'll be going to Charlestown State Prison Monday to inform him that you're filing a petition for divorce, and to ask for his cooperation. If you think it might help to write him a letter, I can bring it to him at that time."

Nell said, "I'll write one and give it to you before you leave."

"Under normal circumstances," the lawyer continued, "I would suggest that you offer him a generous financial settlement—that sometimes does the trick—but given that he has another twenty years to serve on his sentence, I'm not sure money would be a strong enough incentive."

"You can try it," Nell said, "but you're right—I doubt it will make any difference."

"Do you think it would help to mention in the petition that he attacked Nell viciously?" Viola asked.

"Doubtful. It was a long time ago, and it would be difficult to prove. And, too, such incidents are generally viewed as private matters between husbands and wives."

Viola muttered something very unladylike. "The second facilitating factor," she said, "would be the use of influence and bribes, I assume?"

"As always, Viola," Mead chuckled, "your candor is uniquely refreshing. I don't call them bribes, though. I call them 'financial incentives.' "

Imagining herself growing large with child while still wed to Duncan, Nell said, "I'll pay whatever I have to pay."

"That's good to know," Mead said, "but I suspect it won't amount to very much, because of Mrs. Hewitt's connections." Withdrawing a notebook and a steel pen from the wallet pocket of his sleek black dinner coat, he told Viola, "Now would be the time to brag about your friends in high places. I know you're acquainted with Charles Allen, the attorney general, and with Mayor Shurtleff."

"I've met Governor Claflin a few times as well," she said, "and we got along famously. And there are several Boston aldermen and members of the Common Council whose wives I've become friendly with from serving on charity boards. Oh, and there's Horace Bacon, the criminal court judge. His wife is an acquaintance of mine, and I happen to know she's got expensive tastes—more expensive than he can afford on his salary. He's not above accepting the occasional payment for services rendered. I paid him myself a couple of years ago—or rather Nell did, on my behalf, when I was trying to help Will out of a fix he'd got himself in."

Mr. Mead said, "That's good to know, about Bacon, because he's a close friend of Chief Justice Brigham of the Suffolk County Superior Court, which rules on divorce petitions. Anyone else?" he asked. "Anyone who might, perchance, have something to hide?"

"You engage in blackmail, too?" Viola asked with a mock shudder of excitement. "How deliciously low."

"Not blackmail per se," he said, "more like subtle threats—however, such tactics are always a last resort."

"As I recall," Nell said, "Judge Bacon was one of the men who paid Detective Skinner to keep their names out of the investigation into Virginia Kimball's murder last year."

"Charlie Skinner," Mead said with a look of disgust. "Good riddance to that particular piece of human rubbish."

"You know of him?" Nell asked.

"Oh, he had quite the reputation even before the police hearings in February. I was pleased when he was demoted, and delighted when he was kicked off the force altogether."

As if she were a mother bragging about her clever daughter, Viola said with a smile, "His dismissal was due in no small measure to Nell's efforts."

"Well done, Miss Sweeney," Mead praised. "You know, Skinner made himself the enemy of some very important men during those hearings. As you're already aware, he was in the habit of taking bribes.

If a gentleman found himself in a compromising situation—rounded up during a vice raid, say—he would have a nice, thick envelope sent to Charlie Skinner, and next thing you knew there would be no record at all of the arrest. But Skinner never forgot the names of those men, nor the nature of their transgressions, and during the hearings he put pressure on them to clear his name. That turned out to be impossible given his documented history of criminal activity, but he did manage to remain on the force, albeit as a uniformed patrolman. It wouldn't hurt, while I'm trying to garner support for your divorce petition, to mention the fact that you were responsible for Skinner's ouster from the force."

Mr. Mead snapped his notebook shut and returned it to his pocket. "At the risk of giving you false hope, Miss Sweeney, I must say I'm feeling quite optimistic. It helps that your husband is a convicted felon, whereas you are a young lady of sterling reputation with some of the most notable men in the commonwealth vouching for you. The only factor likely to drag things out would be Mr. Sweeney's lack of cooperation. If you can manage to talk him into agreeing to the divorce, I think it's possible you could be a free woman within a matter of weeks."

She gaped at him. "Oh, my God. That would be . . . That would be wonderful." But first she had to talk Duncan into agreeing to it, and that would be much easier said than done.

"I'll go through the process with you in more depth tomorrow," he told her, "and have you sign the papers and so forth. When would be the best time?"

Nell looked to Viola, who said, "August usually takes a nap in the early afternoon. We could meet in my sitting room at, say, two o'clock."

"After I return to Boston," Mead said, "I shall keep in touch. In the interest of discretion, I take it I should address any correspondence to you, Viola, rather than to Miss Sweeney?"

"Yes, do," Viola said. "I'll be making it a point to get to the mail before August does, in order to intercept any communications from Mr. Sweeney or Mr. Skinner, but one can't be too careful. If August were to get wind of this, God knows how he would react."

Oh, thought Nell, *I have a pretty good idea.*

"DR. Greaves had to leave," Martin told Nell as she wheeled his mother into the parlor. "I told him he'd be better off spending the night than driving home in the dark, but he said he had patients to see early tomorrow morning, and that he had a very good carriage lamp. He asked me to apologize on his behalf for not saying good-bye to you."

Dismayed, Nell said, "How long ago did he leave?"

"Just now."

Excusing herself, she lifted her skirts and sprinted through the house and out the front door. She saw a dark figure in a top hat walking away along the lamp-lit path that led to the carriage house. "Cyril!"

He turned, paused, and came back, removing the hat as he climbed the steps of the front porch, bathed in amber lamplight from a large open window into the deserted great hall. "I'm sorry to have left without saying good-bye," he said "but I have some early-morning—"

"I know. Martin told me. I just . . . I wanted to talk to you about what Cecilia said, about Will and I having been engaged."

He dragged a hand through his hair. "Is Duncan . . . Did he die in prison?" he asked.

"No. No, he's still alive. In fact, I'm petitioning for a divorce. That's what Mr. Mead and Mrs. Hewitt and I were talking about just now. If I can get Duncan to agree to it, which I hope to God I can, Mr. Mead says the divorce might come through in just a few weeks."

Cyril, looking baffled, said, "If you've been married all this time, how could you and William Hewitt have been engaged?"

"There *was* no engagement," she said. "That's what I wanted to tell you. It was all pretense, to provide a rationale for . . . the closeness of our friendship. Otherwise, we were afraid people would have thought I was his mistress."

"You aren't?"

The question took Nell aback for a moment, until she realized it wasn't disrespect that had prompted it, but the natural curiosity of a man for whom she had once served in that very capacity. "No, I'm not, but people were starting to suspect that I was. It was generally assumed that *I* was the only reason he spent so much time with Gracie and me. I was part of the reason, but he also wanted to see Gracie."

Cyril pondered that for about a second, and then a look of revelation came over his face. "Of course. *Of course.* I'd always wondered why a Brahmin matron would be so eager to adopt the child of a chambermaid."

"Viola Hewitt is no ordinary Brahmin matron. She's a born iconoclast. I've often thought she might have adopted Gracie even if Will hadn't fathered her."

Leaning on the stone balustrade, arms crossed, Cyril said, "Does Gracie know he's her father?"

Nell shook her head. "He won't let us tell her. He thinks it would just bring her misery."

"Because she's illegitimate? She's too young to understand the concept, and by the time she's old enough, she'll almost certainly have figured it out herself. Most adopted children were born out of wedlock."

"It's not that. He thinks she'll be ashamed that her father is . . ." Oh blast, why had she allowed the conversation to veer down this particular path?

"A gambler and an opium smoker?"

"He doesn't smoke it anymore," she said quickly, hating the notion of Cyril viewing Will that way. "He hasn't in two and a half years. Well, except for once, when he was . . . he'd just found out I was married, and that I'd kept it from him. He . . . he was upset." *I thought you trusted me. I thought you knew me. I thought we were friends.* "And, um, he did it once in Shanghai a few months ago, but he was in a very melancholic frame of—"

"Shanghai?"

Nell just sighed. How could one rationalize Shanghai? There was no greater haven of sin in the world. "He really is through with opium," she said, declining to mention that he'd weaned himself off it by injecting morphine, on which he'd been dependent for another half year.

"Nell, I wish I could share your confidence, but from what you've just told me, he doesn't seem to be able to resist the lure of Morpheus for very long. Whenever he's feeling out of sorts, he goes right back to it."

"It doesn't have its talons in him the way it used to," she said. "When I first met Will, he was . . . ravaged. He'd had a miserable upbringing in England, after having been torn away from his mother at a young age because Mr. Hewitt couldn't deal with him. Andersonville was a nightmare. He saw his brother murdered, for which he blamed himself, and then he escaped after taking a bullet in the leg—but his parents were told he'd died of dysentery. He spent nine months making his way back north through enemy territory, using opium just so he could stay on his feet. After the war, he was alienated from his family, haunted by his memories, and still in constant pain. He literally didn't care whether he lived or died. But that's all changing. He's a different man now. I can't imagine him ever using opiates again."

"I have no doubt he must be a good man at heart, to have earned your esteem, but from what I've been able to gather, he doesn't seem to have changed as much as you would like to think. Men don't go to Shanghai for cultural fulfillment, Nell, they go there to steep themselves in depravity. He won't commit to Harvard, won't commit to being a real father to Gracie . . ."

"It's complicated," she said. "*He's* complicated."

"So was Duncan."

Appalled that he would make such a comparison, Nell said, "Will is nothing like Duncan—*nothing*." Her hard tone of voice surprised her; she'd never once spoken in anger to Cyril Greaves.

Cyril looked surprised, too—and chastened. Pushing off the balustrade to take a step in her direction, he said, "Of course he isn't. I had no business saying that. Please put it out of your mind."

Nell nodded pensively.

She thought he would bid her good night then, but instead he said, a little hesitantly, "Viola . . . She took me aside before dinner. She's worried about you, Nell. She said you became violently ill a few days ago, and she heard you being sick again yesterday. I told her I'd seen you growing faint. She has, too. She wants me to examine you."

"I don't need to be examined," Nell said. "I'm not ill."

"Just the heat, eh?"

"I'm fine, really. I'm sorry Viola has been fretting over me. The next time you're here, please tell her there's nothing wrong with me."

"The next time? Does that mean you want me to come back?"

"Of course I do. I do, Cyril. I'm enjoying getting to know you again."

"And I you. Well." He put his hat back on. "I suppose I should be going. Good night, Nell."

"Good night."

He set out again for the carriage house, his shoes crunching on the gravel drive. A bit too shaky to go inside and face everyone quite yet, Nell sat on the stone bench beneath the window, hugged a little needlepoint pillow to her chest, and closed her eyes, listening to his footsteps retreat into the night.

When they were almost inaudible, they abruptly ceased. There was no sound at all for about a full minute, and then the crunching started again, growing louder this time as Cyril retraced his steps. He climbed back up onto the porch, took his hat off, and came to stand before her.

"I'd like you to marry me," he said.

She stared at him.

"If and when your divorce comes through, of course," he added.

She could not find her tongue.

"May I?" he asked, gesturing toward the bench.

She nodded.

He sat next to her. "Nell, I know when a woman is suffering from the heat, and I know when she's with child."

Shaken, Nell scrambled for a response. Realizing in short order that she was blushing and flustered, she strove to school her features, but it was, of course, too late.

"It's true, then," he said. "I thought so. The nausea and dizziness, the loss of appetite. Your eagerness to be divorced as soon as possible . . ."

"Do . . . Oh, dear God. Do you think Viola suspects?"

"If she does, she's keeping it to herself. Does Will know?" He didn't even question who the baby's father was.

She shook her head. Looking up at him, she said, "I wasn't lying when I told you I'm not his mistress. It wasn't like that. It was . . . just once, before he took ship."

"Yes, well, he should have taken precautions."

"I didn't think it was necessary. I thought I was . . . You told me I was probably barren after the miscarriage, so . . ."

"*Probably*, not definitely." With a wry smile, he said, "Of course, you never conceived, so I suppose we both assumed . . . But it would appear that I was the infertile one, eh?"

This was the first time since the renewal of their acquaintance that either of them had made reference, even obliquely, to the physical intimacy they had once shared. It was as if they'd had an unspoken agreement to pretend that part of their past hadn't existed—until now.

Cyril propped his elbows on his knees and rubbed the brim of his hat between his fingers. "I've always felt a genuine affection for you, Nell, and a great deal of respect. You have a giving heart, or you never would have . . . indulged me as you once did. It was a gesture of kindness on your part, but one which I should never have asked of you."

"Cyril . . ."

"Please let me say this, Nell," he said without looking up. "I've wanted to say this for a long time. When I met you, you'd been savagely abused, you had no place to go. I offered you the protection of my home, and then I . . ." He shook his head.

"You're making it sound as if you took advantage of me," she said. "It wasn't like that."

"In hindsight, I'm not so sure." Turning his head to look at her, he said quietly, "Let me do this for you, Nell. I'll acknowledge your baby as mine, and I'll take good care of both of you. We can live in Boston, if you like, so that you can be close to Gracie." Looking down again, he said, "If, um, if you prefer, we can have separate bedrooms, and I promise I won't expect . . . anything of that nature. And if, after the baby comes, you choose to divorce me, I won't contest it or make things difficult for you. All I want is to take care of you, and to legitimize your baby. If you give birth out of wedlock, your life will be ruined. I can't let that happen, not after all that's transpired between us."

Bombarded by conflicting emotions, Nell said, "I don't know what to say, Cyril. What you're offering is incredibly generous, but I . . . I . . ."

"Has he ever mentioned marriage? Did he offer you any kind of commitment or promise at all before he . . ."

"As far as he knew at the time, as far as we both knew, marriage was impossible because Duncan was threatening to ruin me if I divorced him. That's all changed, but at the time . . ."

"Has he told you he loves you?"

He hadn't, even that night. "You have to understand, our relationship had been so . . . so careful for so long. We never talked about how we felt. He was always guarded in what he said and did—for my sake, because I had so much at stake. He only went to France to put some distance between us, because it was so excruciating, our being together but . . . not being together. The night we . . . It wasn't supposed to happen, but it did. For him to declare himself when he couldn't offer me any kind of commitment would have just made the situation more painful for both of us."

"That is a great deal of explanation for a very simple question, Nell." Before she could summon a response to that, he said, "Do you love him?"

Nell closed her eyes and nodded.

"Nell, you told me the other day that you have no way of knowing when he might be back from the war, that it could be months or years."

She nodded morosely.

"You understand that by the time he comes back, your life will be utterly destroyed—if you've remained unwed."

"I know." She took his hand. It was a kind offer, and a tempting one. Cyril Greaves was a good man, she'd always been fond of him. "If I could have some time to think about it . . ."

"Of course. I'll stay away till you've made your decision. When you know what you want to do, just send me a message, and I'll meet you anywhere you'd like. And I meant it when I said I'd moved to Boston. I'll do whatever it takes to make you happy."

"You're a remarkable man, Cyril." She hugged him and kissed his cheek, noticing, as she drew away, a movement through the window. Martin was pushing his mother's wheelchair into the great hall, both of them turning to look in Nell's direction as she looked in theirs. Nell recoiled, seeing, from Martin and Viola's perspective, the intimate little tête-à-tête on the darkened porch, the embrace, the kiss.

Martin turned and wheeled his mother out of the room with impressive nonchalance, as if it had nothing to do with what he'd just seen. The window was raised; had they heard anything? *If I could have some time to think about it . . . I'll stay away till you've made your decision.*

She groaned as Cyril gathered her in his arms and patted her back. "Why," she muttered into his chest, "does everything always have to get so . . . so *damned* complicated?"

He chuckled, no doubt because of the awkward and self-conscious way in which she swore; he used to tease her about that. "The world is complicated, Nell. People are complicated. If that weren't so, life would get pretty *damned* boring."

Chapter 5

"LATE afternoon is my favorite time of day," said Viola as she sat on the front porch at the top of the steps, gazing across acres of rolling lawn terminating in the majestic wrought iron gate at the edge of the road. Were it not for the fingers of her right hand, tapping incessantly on the arm of her wheelchair, she would have seemed completely at ease. "I love it when the sun is low in the sky and the shadows are long. Have you ever noticed how vibrant colors look at this hour?"

Nell, sitting on the stone bench with the sleeping

Gracie's head on her lap and Clancy reclining at her feet, looked up from yesterday's *New York Herald*, rumpled from numerous readings and rereadings. The grass was richly green, the sky an unearthly blue streaked with gold-rimmed clouds. "It's exquisite. I'd like to paint a landscape with that kind of light."

Four days had passed since Viola saw Nell and Cyril embracing on the porch. Ever the circumspect Brit, Viola hadn't mentioned the incident or whether she'd overheard anything of the tail end of their conversation. Nell hoped she'd been too far away to hear, if for no other reason than Viola's explicit desire that Nell remain unwed while Gracie was young. Nell had, after all, told Cyril that she would consider his proposal.

She *had* considered it. She'd lain awake considering it. She'd spent hours sorting through her dilemma, but every time she came to the conclusion that marrying Cyril was her only prudent option, she would think about Will and what they'd shared and feel a terrible sense of wrongness at the notion of standing at the altar with Cyril.

"Doesn't it seem as if he should be back already?" Viola snapped open her little diamond-encrusted pocket watch and held it close to her eyes, squinting; it amused Nell that she refused to get reading spectacles.

"Don't forget, he had to go to the Western Union office as well as to the depot. He'll be back soon."

Nell scanned the front page one more time, looking for some detail she might not have noticed before, some clue as to how Will may have fared during last Thursday's crushing defeat of Napoleon's forces at Wissembourg.

THE WAR.

Highly Important News From the Field.

Marshal MacMahon Defeated by the Prussians.

The French Vigorously Assailed and Driven Back.

Napoleon's Despatches Acknowledging His Defeat.

The German Army Said to Be Marching on Paris.

The article itself was frustratingly sketchy, providing no details of the battle or its aftermath, just that it had occurred at Wissembourg. The reason for this dearth of information was explained by a statement toward the bottom of the page: *The strictest surveillance is exercised by the French government over telegraphs and telegraphic communication on all sides.* With any luck, there would be better coverage in today's edition of the *Herald*, which Brady would be bringing back from the Falmouth train depot. Hopefully he would also have an overseas cable from Mr. Carlisle, an old college friend of August Hewitt's who was with the diplomatic service in London.

Yesterday evening, a Western Union boy had come by with a telegram for Viola from Mr. Hewitt in Boston: *As reports of Wissembourg must worry you, and cannot communicate with Paris, have cabled Reggie Carlisle to make enquiries at our embassy in London. Perhaps Americans fleeing Paris will have news of William. Carlisle will reply to you as well as to me. August.* Given the enmity between Viola's husband and firstborn son, Nell was surprised that Mr. Hewitt had gone to such trouble. She might think his concern was solely for his wife, had he not asked his old friend to cable his reply to *both* of them.

"You're positive Will was there?" Viola asked.

"In his cable, he said he was to 'join Marshal MacMahon's I Corps near Wissembourg on the German border.' "

Viola propped her elbow on the arm of her wheelchair and rubbed her temple. "I still don't understand why he went over there. It's not our fight. I realize it's hard to deny a request of the president, but when one is talking about risking one's . . ."

She sat upright, staring across the lawn. "He's back."

Gently lifting Gracie's head from her lap, Nell laid it on the needlepoint pillow; the child grunted softly, but never awoke. Nell stood and crossed to the edge of the stairs accompanied by Clancy. She shielded her eyes as she peered at the gatehouse in the distance, from which Michael and Liam emerged to haul open the gate for the Hewitts' family brougham. The gleaming black coach crawled toward them with agonizing slowness, veering off toward the carriage house when the path forked, instead of coming directly to the house.

With a groan of exasperation, Nell bounded down the stairs and across the lawn with the poodle tearing along beside her, yipping excitedly. "Brady!"

He reined in the horses and lifted an envelope and

a folded-up newspaper from the seat next to him, handing them down to Nell when she approached. "Sorry, dear. I shoulda known you wouldn't want to wait for these."

She brought them back to the porch, handing Viola the envelope, which was imprinted WESTERN UNION and addressed to her. And then she opened the *Herald* to the front page.

DETAILS OF THE BATTLE OF WISSEMBOURG.

King William Anxious for Action—The Assault on the French Outpost and Its Results.

LONDON, August 8, 1870.

A special correspondent writes from Mayence on Thursday:—

This evening came a despatch from Wissembourg, announcing a Prussian victory and the occupation of Wissembourg. I have seen the official despatch and obtained the following additional details:—

The King, on his arrival at Mayence, called a council of war and urged that the sooner the existing infiltration ceased the better, and pressed an advance. His opinion was adopted and orders telegraphed to attack the French outposts in the neighborhood of Landau and Wissembourg.

A Prussian force composed of two line regiments, one regiment of Bavarian troops and some artillery, together about 9,000 strong, drove the French before them into Wissembourg.

The artillery was then brought up and opened on the fortifications of the town. The town soon caught fire. Seeing this and some confusion among the French troops, the Prussians could no longer be restrained by their officers, who were anxious to reduce the town by cannonade.

The soldiers rushed forward with bayonets and surprised the French, who, not expecting an infantry attack for hours to come, were barricading and entrenching. The Prussians lost heavily, but took 800 prisoners and the town. The greatest enthusiasm prevails here, and there is an Immense crowd about the Palace waiting to cheer the King.

The same correspondent wires from Mayence, Friday midnight:—

Half the prisoners taken at Wissembourg were first marched from the citadel to the railway.

The French had lost 2,300 killed, wounded, and prisoners.

"Dear God, please protect him," Nell whispered. Perhaps, she thought, he hadn't left for Wissembourg after all. Or perhaps he'd gotten away before the Prussians ravaged the town. But then she recalled what Jack Thorpe had told her of Will's valor during the War between the States, particularly at the Battle of Olustee in Florida. *He was fearless, took insane risks, exposed himself to enemy fire time and again to retrieve wounded men. He saved a great many lives before he was captured.*

He would never have been taken prisoner at all had he not insisted on remaining behind when his unit retreated from Olustee. *The battle was ending,* Jack had said. *Robbie was injured—badly, he couldn't be moved. Will wouldn't leave him. There were some other wounded men, too, but I knew it was Robbie he didn't want to leave. He stayed with them and let himself be captured.*

Chances were slim that Will would have left the town of Wissembourg while there were still men there who needed him. If he *had* managed to get away, where would he have gone? Back to Paris? According to the *Herald*, the city was in a state of bedlam.

The Situation in Paris Most Critical for Napoleon—Shame and Humiliation at the Army Defeats—At the Point of Revolution.

LONDON, August 8, 1870.

The news from Paris grows hourly more serious. None but official accounts can come by telegraph. It is from letters and Paris journals that all intelligence must be gathered. The declaration of the state of siege does not repress popular demonstrations, and it is very doubtful whether the government has force to keep order or to put down any considerable demonstrations. The Republicans believe that their hour approaches, and Paris at the moment is as likely to rise against Napoleon as to arm against Prussia.

Skimming the rest of that article, Nell said, "It doesn't look good, Mrs. Hewitt. The situation in

Paris is getting worse. And at Wissembourg, eight hundred French soldiers were taken prisoner, and fifteen hundred others were killed or wounded."

Nell looked up from the paper to find Viola sitting with the telegram open on her lap, gazing vacantly into the distance; she looked strangely old and drawn. "Mrs. Hewitt? Is that cable from Mr. Carlisle?"

Viola nodded and handed it to Nell. Written in a slapdash hand on the lined Western Union form was the message: *Spoke to clerk from Paris Embassy now in London who was told I Corps lost their surgeon, Dr. Hewitt, at Wissembourg. Not sure whether captured or killed, hopefully former. Am so terribly sorry. Will pray for him. R. Carlisle.*

"Oh, my God." Nell sat on the bench and read the cable a second time, and a third, as if the words written there might re-form themselves into a more benign meaning if only she scrutinized them long enough. "Oh, my God."

"What was he doing there?" Viola demanded in a quavering voice. "I *cannot* comprehend it. He had no business being there. Why did he go?"

He went there because of me, thought Nell as she buried her head in her hands. *It was all because of me.*

Chapter 6

"ISN'T that your Dr. Greaves?" asked Eileen, looking toward the house as she sat at the edge of the bay with Gracie, building a sand castle.

Nell, standing at her easel nearby, turned to find Cyril crossing the lawn, his hand raised in greeting. Eileen and Gracie waved back, as did Nell, wondering what he was doing here. The last time she'd seen him, just over two weeks ago, he'd told her he would stay away until she'd decided whether to accept his offer of marriage.

Gracie, her damp bathing dress frosted with

sand, got up and ran over to him as he strode across the beach. "Come look at my sand castle, Dr. Gweaves!"

"Greaves," Nell corrected.

"Can I call you Cywil instead?" she asked him. "I mean, *Cyril*?"

Nell said, "No, you may not. It wouldn't be respectful."

"But *you* call him that."

"Because he asked me to."

"How about *Uncle* Cyril?" he suggested. "I know I'm not actually your uncle, but it strikes me as an acceptable compromise."

"Uncle Will's not weally my . . . *really* my uncle, either, but I call him 'Uncle,' too. Can I, Miseeny?"

"Yes, you *may*," she replied, whereupon the delighted child grabbed "Uncle Cyril's" hand and dragged him over to her sand castle, upon which he heaped munificent praise. Rejoining Nell, he nodded toward the paint-crusted tunic she wore over her black-dyed shirtwaist and skirt. "That smock looks to have done you yeoman's service."

"I've had it for years."

"What are you painting?"

She stepped aside so that he could have a good

view of the canvas, which depicted Waquoit Bay beneath a dense slab of storm clouds, executed mostly in shades of lead, pewter, and slate.

"Not painting from life?" he asked, looking around at the cloudless midday sky and glassy bay.

She said, "I started it about a week and a half ago, when the bay really looked like this. I've just been polishing it since then." Or rather, ruining it. Disinclined to declare the painting finished, for some reason, she'd reworked it to the point where it just looked stilted and muddy and dead.

"I hope the tone of this painting doesn't reflect your state of mind regarding . . ." He looked toward Gracie and Eileen, industriously molding towers from empty flowerpots. "You know. What we discussed the last time I was here." His proposal, he meant.

"No, of course not," she assured him. "Not remotely. If I've been in a black mood, it's been . . . for another reason entirely." Not wanting Gracie to hear the reason for her despondency, Nell asked Cyril if he wouldn't help her haul her equipment back to the house.

When they were out of earshot of the child, he carrying her easel and paint box and she the wet painting, she told him about Will being unaccounted for after the Battle of Wissembourg.

"We keep hoping we'll hear from him, or at least *of* him, but so far . . . not a word."

"God, Nell, I'm sorry," he said earnestly. "How awful not to know what happened to him. Isn't there any way—"

"Paris is in a state of chaos," she said. "There are no cables going in or out except for official French dispatches. I believe the American Embassy is still functioning, but there's no way to contact them, and even if we could, who's to say they even know what happened to Will?"

Cyril said, "I truly hate to burden you with this when you've so much on your mind, but I have some new information about your brother."

Nell stopped walking at the edge of the flagstone court behind the house. "What information?"

"I was leaving the East Falmouth post office yesterday, when who should I run into but Warren Leatherby."

"Why do I know that name?"

"Chief Bryce mentioned him. He's the county coroner. I've had to deal with him from time to time, so I recognized him. I told him I had an interest in the Cunningham case, particularly as re-garded James Murphy, so we chatted for a few min-utes. It seems he's quite put out with Chief Bryce and his 'provincial ineptitude.' He's particularly irate because his report following Dr. Monk's post-mortem on your brother, which interpreted Monk's findings for forensic purposes, was all but ignored by Bryce."

"Did he tell you what was in the report?"

"I asked. He told me Dr. Monk's autopsy notes were perfunctory in the extreme, but that he had noted a nick on the left fourth rib."

"A nick?"

"As if from a blade of some sort."

"Could Dr. Monk have made that mark himself, during the course of the autopsy?" Nell asked.

"Leatherby questioned him about that, but he in-sisted the only tool that had come anywhere near the ribs was the scalpel used to make the Y incision."

"That isn't possible," Nell said. "He would have needed a bone saw or shears to cut through the ribs."

"He didn't cut through the ribs."

Nell stared at Cyril for a moment, wondering if she'd heard him right. "He didn't remove the chest plate? Then how could he have examined the organs?"

"He didn't," Cyril said. "My guess is he cut the body open to make it look as if it had been properly autopsied, in case anyone checked, but then he just sewed it back up so as not to damage the merchandise before it was delivered to Harvard."

Nell shook her head in dismay.

Cyril said, "He did notice that nicked rib, which he concluded was a souvenir from some long-ago knife fight."

"One that my brother would have been unlikely to survive," Nell said, "seeing as the left fourth rib is pretty much directly over the heart."

"Leatherby—who's a lawyer, but seems to know more about human physiology than Monk—made that point in his report, but he said Chief Bryce completely dismissed it. Bryce told him if a surgeon said it was from a knife fight, that was good enough for him. It goes without saying that Bryce has no desire to investigate alternate theories as to how your brother might have died. He's in over his head, and he knows it. He just wants this case to go away as quickly as possible."

"So Jamie may not have actually died in that fire," she said. "He may have died from a knife to the chest."

"Not that we'll ever know for sure, given Bryce's disinterest in finding out what really happened."

"*I'm* not disinterested," Nell said. "If my brother was deliberately murdered, I want to know why and how. I want to know who did it. I want to know what I can do about it."

"My avenging angel," Cyril said with a smile.

My? "Jamie was my brother," she said gravely. "Who better to avenge him than me?"

She ushered him into the greenhouse-turned-studio and put away her gear while he perused her paintings.

"Your work is remarkable," he said. "You've made extraordinary progress. Your light . . . it shimmers."

"Mrs. Hewitt has taken me under her wing. She studied painting in Paris when she was young."

Leafing through one of her sketchbooks, he said, a bit too casually, "Any news about the status of your divorce petition?"

"Mr. Mead has written to me a couple of times. His visit to Duncan went much as I thought it would.

Duncan was surly, and refused to sign the papers. Mr. Mead gave him my letter and his business card before he left. He begged him to reconsider, and asked him to write if he did."

"Do you think he might?"

"I pray that he will." Hanging up her smock, she said, "Mr. Mead said it will take a good deal longer for the divorce to come through if Duncan contests it. I stayed up half the night composing that letter to Duncan. I was completely frank. I told him that I'm expecting, and that I'll be ruined if I can't remarry soon."

"Do you think that was prudent?"

"I don't have time for prudence, Cyril. I'm more than a month along. I told him that I trust him with this information because of everything we've been through. I asked him, if he has a spark of true affection left for me, to search within himself for the gallantry I know is there and release me from my marriage bonds. And I . . . I told him I forgive him for . . . what he did to me."

"*Do* you?" Cyril asked incredulously.

"I think I actually do. For years, I've prayed for God's help in learning to forgive him, but I couldn't.

He'd taken my baby from me, the only baby I thought I'd never have. But now . . ."

She rested a hand on her stomach, remembering the words she had struggled over during those long, candlelit hours. *God hasn't just given me another baby, Duncan, he's given me the grace to forgive you. The bitterness that had burdened me all those years is gone. It's like a thousand-ton weight off my shoulders.*

"Now that darkness, that hate, is all part of the past," she said. "I can put it behind me and move on."

"ARE you expecting another guest, Viola?" asked August Hewitt as he sat on the front porch late that afternoon enjoying a preprandial sherry with his wife, Nell, and Cyril, who had been coaxed into staying for supper.

They followed his gaze across the lawn to a hackney passing through the front gate. As it neared Gracie, who was throwing a stick to Clancy about fifty yards from the house, the driver reined in his horses. Gracie paused to look in the hack's direction as its door opened.

The stick dropped from her hand. She shrieked and raced toward the hack as a tall man in a black frock coat and fawn trousers stepped down from it, took off his low-crowned top hat, and opened his arms.

"Oh, my God," whispered Viola.

Gathering up her skirts, Nell dashed down the porch steps and across the lawn.

Will, kneeling in the grass to embrace his daughter, looked up as she joined them, breathless and shaking. He stood, a bit stiffly because of that old bullet wound, and pushed an errant lock of black hair off his forehead as he smiled into her eyes. "God, Nell, I can't tell you how good it is to see you." His voice, so achingly familiar—deep and resonant, with a lingering accent from his many years in England—was barely audible over the pounding in her ears.

"Will." She wanted to throw herself into his arms, but mindful of their audience on the porch, she maintained a suitable distance. "We thought you were . . . We were told that I Corps lost their surgeon at Wissembourg."

"Which was true, but open to interpretation, I suppose." Taking in her afternoon dress of gauzy black melrose, he said, "Please don't tell me you're in mourning for *me*."

"Oh. No. My . . . my brother, Jamie . . . He died about three weeks ago."

"Oh, Nell. I am so sorry."

"Nana's cwying," said Gracie as she cradled Clancy in her arms.

Looking toward the house, Nell saw Cyril, standing next to Viola at the top of the steps, hand her a handkerchief. This wasn't the first time her eldest son had been resurrected after she thought she'd lost him.

"She's happy," Nell told the child. "Everyone is happy to see Uncle Will."

As she said that, August Hewitt opened the front door and disappeared inside.

"Not quite everyone." Will paid the driver, retrieved his old alligator physician's satchel and traveling case, and accompanied Nell and Gracie back to the porch. He kissed his mother's tearstained cheek and extended his hand to Cyril as Nell introduced them. "It's good to meet you at last. Nell has spoken highly of you."

"Same here."

Nell had the impression, as the two men shook

hands, that their gazes were connecting just a bit too intently, as if they were taking each other's measure.

Once he was settled on the porch with a glass of sherry, Will explained that he'd suffered an injury to his right arm during the battle, whereupon Marshall Patrice MacMahon, who commanded Napoleon's I Corps, declared him unfit to perform surgery and excused him from further service. "I managed to give Wilhelm's boys the slip before they started rounding up prisoners," he said. "I got out of Wissembourg and was transported to Calais, where I found passage on a mail packet bound for Boston. I arrived yesterday."

Cyril, ever the physician, asked Will how he'd sustained the injury, to which Will replied that he'd "had a bit too much absinthe and took a spill." He met Nell's gaze and smiled. She smiled back; it wasn't the first time he'd used that absinthe line.

"Perhaps you should let me have a look at it," Cyril suggested.

"Uncle Cyril is a doctor, too," Gracie told him as she sat on the floor cradling Clancy.

Will lifted his glass and took a sip, his eyes dark, jaw slightly outthrust—although Nell was probably the only one who noticed. She wondered if it was because his daughter had bestowed avuncular status, once reserved solely for him, on the interloper Cyril Greaves. He said, "It's actually an embarrassingly minor wound—as you can see, I've full use of the arm—but it does make my hand a bit unsteady, which is why I can't do surgery."

Viola said, "You look exhausted, Will." It was true. His gaze was somnolent, and his skin had a washed-out translucence that made him look almost consumptive.

"War is an even more unpleasant pastime than I had recalled," he said dryly. "And, too, I've been on the move for over two weeks, in less than luxurious circumstances. Getting to Calais was a trial all by itself, and that packet was a rusted-out old bucket, barely seaworthy. I'd never been seasick in my life till that crossing."

"Falconwood is the perfect place to rejuvenate yourself," Viola told him. "You must stay here with us till you've got your bearings."

"I must admit," he said, "I was counting on just such an invitation. It might be best, however, if I took up residence in the boathouse, as I did when I was young." It was to avoid the inevitable altercations with Mr. Hewitt that Will used to stay alone in the boathouse during family summers on the Cape. And, too, he once told Nell he that found the lapping of the water restful.

"Of course," Viola said. "I'll have a bed made up for you there. Stay as long as you need to. We'll be leaving at the end of the month, but you're welcome to remain here if you like."

"We shall see," he said with a glance at Nell.

"Mrs. Waters must have known you were coming," his mother told him. "She's making wild duck with onion sauce for supper."

"It's probably best if I take my meals in the kitchen, as I used to," he said. "Less familial drama to spoil everyone's appetites."

"Your father is going to be here for the rest of the month," Viola said. "I hate to think of you eating all your meals alone."

"I'll eat with him!" Gracie said. "Can I, Miseeny? I mean, *may* I?"

Nell looked to Will, who said, "I'd be delighted to have the company."

"Very well—but young ladies who've been playing fetch with dogs must wash up and put on clean frocks before they eat." Nell stood and reached for Gracie's hand.

"I'll see to it," said Viola as she wheeled over to the door, which Will held open for her. "Come along, Gracie. You, too, Clancy."

Nell, Will, and Cyril sat in awkward silence for a few moments, until Nell said, "Will is an expert in forensics, Cyril. I don't know whether I've mentioned that."

"You have, yes," Cyril said. "A fascinating specialty, Hewitt."

"*I* think so," Will said.

"The Falmouth coroner could use someone like you," Nell said. "He's got a real quack doing postmortems for him."

"Nell's brother died under suspicious circumstances," Cyril told Will. He explained about Jamie's fugitive status, the fire, the slapdash autopsy, and the uselessness of the Falmouth constabulary.

"The first thing that's needed," Will said, "if one really wants to get to the bottom of this, is a competent autopsy."

"But he's already been buried," Nell said.

"Bodies *can* be exhumed," Will said, "and as Jamie's next of kin, yours would be the only permission required. His having been embalmed is all for the good. Not that I'd be too deft with the scalpel right now."

"I could handle that end of it," Cyril told him. "Of course, I wouldn't mind if you were there to lend your expertise."

"Are you seriously suggesting this?" Nell asked.

"If it would put your mind at ease, why not?" Will asked. "Unless you find the notion of disturbing your brother's remains too troubling to—"

"What I find troubling," she said, "is suspecting that Jamie's been murdered, but not being able to prove it. If you two are willing to conduct a proper postmortem, then yes, I would very much appreciate it. I also wouldn't mind going to the farm where he died and speaking to this Claire Gilmartin and her mother. I'd like to find out if anyone knew Jamie was there, or if any strangers had been seen lurking about."

"Today is Saturday," Cyril said. "You won't be able to apply for the exhumation till Monday. You'll have to go to the Falmouth Town Hall for that. I'd do it for you, but I have appointments all day."

Will told her that he would accompany her to Falmouth Monday morning, and then to the

Gilmartin farm. When dinner was announced, he took his leave and went out back to the boathouse with his satchel and traveling case.

Cyril held the front door open for Nell. As she was passing by him, he stilled her with a hand on her arm and said quietly, "I want you to know that my offer of marriage still stands."

THAT night, after the rest of the household was asleep, Nell buttoned her wrapper over her night shift and stole out of the house on slippered feet through the French doors in the dining room. She sprinted down the back porch steps and across the lawn to the boathouse, through which lamplight glowed in the windows.

The second-floor guest suite was accessed through an exterior stone staircase. This she climbed, knocking at the door on the landing. There was no answer. She knocked again, harder. Upon hearing no movement from within, she turned the doorknob, finding it unlocked.

The sitting room that formed the core of the suite was spacious and warmly decorated, with a great deal of leather and polished wood. To the right was a little kitchen, to the left, the stairwell that led upstairs to the turret and downstairs to the boat slips. Straight ahead was the closed door to the bedroom, which was where she assumed Will was, although she couldn't imagine why he'd gone to bed with a lamp lit in the sitting room.

She knocked softly on the bedroom door, waited a moment, and slowly opened it. By the light of a single candle on the dressing table, she saw that the big four-poster bed was not only unoccupied, but tidily made up. The French doors that let out onto the veranda overlooking the bay stood open, but the veranda itself was small enough that Nell could see he wasn't there. From the darkness outside came the rhythmic slapping of waves against the shore.

His open satchel sat on the dressing table alongside a stack of journals and books and the Wedgwood perfume tray that Viola kept there for guests. The tray held a roll of cotton wool, a teacup, several little bottles, and a flat, rectangular brass case.

Nell stared at the tray from across the room, her scalp prickling. With a sense of dread, she crossed to the dressing table, lifted a square-sided cobalt blue bottle, and read its label by the shuddering candlelight.

CARBOLIC ACID
Poison
8 oz.

A smaller, unlabeled bottle was half filled with a clear solution. Next to it was a little vial with a handwritten label that contained a white powder.

Sulfate de Morphine
1 gramme

"Oh, God." Nell lifted the teacup to peer inside, instantly recognizing the tarlike smell of carbolic, of which there was about half an inch in the bottom, with a hypodermic needle soaking in it for purposes of sterilization. She knew what was in the brass case, but she opened it anyway. Snugged into specially shaped niches in its red velveteen lining were a steel-and-glass syringe and three of the four needles that belonged there.

"Damn you, Will." She snapped the case shut, her heart like a chunk of lead in her chest.

He doesn't seem to be able to resist the lure of Morpheus for very long. Whenever he's feeling out of sorts, he goes right back to it.

Will had made light of what he'd been through—*War is an even more unpleasant pastime than I had recalled*—but it would seem his experience in France and the grueling journey home had taken a toll on his state of mind.

Through the open glass doors, Nell saw a tiny flame ignite briefly in the darkness, then wink out. Stepping out onto the veranda and peering into the nearly moonless night, she could just make out the dock extending into the bay, and the raised platform at the end of it. As she watched, there came a minuscule orange glow, as of a cigarette being drawn on. Will rarely smoked anymore, only when he was feeling ill at ease.

Nell left the boathouse using the front staircase rather than the rear one connecting the veranda to the dock, so that Will wouldn't see her. She stood at the bottom of the steps for a minute, her arms wrapped around herself although it was a balmy night. Turning, she walked around the side of the boathouse and down the dock. As she neared the platform, she could make out the two wicker rocking chairs turned toward the water. Will's head was visible above the fan-shaped back of the chair on the left; in his right hand, draped over the side of the chair, the cigarette still glowed.

He didn't hear her until she stepped up onto the platform, and then he turned and saw her. He stood, hurling his cigarette into the bay, and strode up to her, lifting her off her feet as he took her in his arms. His mouth closed over hers for a hot, sweet, lingering kiss that robbed her of her breath, her thoughts, her qualms. He was in his shirtsleeves, the warmth of his body through the thin linen making her heart race. The joy she felt to be holding him again, after agonizing over his fate for twelve long days, was pure and all-consuming.

He set her on her feet, his arms still banded around her. "I want to make love to you." She realized his morphine consumption must not be as high as it had been back in 'sixty-eight, if he'd retained his sexual appetite; that was something.

"Will . . ."

"Just tonight," he said, nuzzling her hair. "And I swear I'll try to back away after that. I don't want to made things difficult for you, I just—"

"It isn't that." *Tell him about the baby. Tell him*

you're trying to get a divorce. It was what she'd come here for.

Until she'd seen that little vial of morphine, those malevolently glinting needles.

"Then let me take you inside," he murmured into her hair as he started unbuttoning her wrapper. "Let me—"

"Not here," she said. "Not with your family so close."

"They're three hundred yards away, fast asleep behind closed doors."

"I just . . . I . . . I . . ."

"Shh, it's all right," he said, pushing the buttons back into their holes. "I'm sorry, Nell. I'm being a selfish cad. You're grieving for your brother, and all I can think about is . . ." He kissed her hair and stepped back. "God, I'm just so happy to see you again."

"Me, too."

"Sit with me?" he said, indicating the rocking chairs.

"Of course."

Will held her chair for her, then pulled his close to hers and sat, both of them facing the water, which was all but invisible. From the corner of her eye, she could see his sharply carved profile, his heavy-lidded eyes.

Presently he said, "There's no sound quite as soothing as the rhythm of waves against the shore—or the hull of a boat. I miss sailing."

"You sail?" He'd never mentioned it.

"I used to. I used to love it. Have you ever done it?"

"No."

"You'd like it. Being out on the water always felt so . . . pure, so clean and invigorating. I'd go out for hours, sometimes days."

"Days?"

"It was how I got out of myself, renewed myself. At night, I'd drop anchor and strip down and swim, or sometimes just float on my back and stare at the stars and think about the future. The present and the past . . . well, there was never any salvaging that, but there always seemed to be such promise just around the next sunrise . . . But that was before—you know—the war and all that."

"You haven't been sailing since the war?"

"No time for daydreaming about the future when you're grappling with the here and now. But you know all about that." Reaching for her hand, he said,

"I truly am sorry about Jamie, Nell. I know how it feels to lose a brother, but at least Robbie and I were always close, and there was some comfort in that. To lose a family member from whom one has been estranged is exceptionally painful, I think, because the emotions are so much more complicated. How long had it been . . . I'm sorry. I'm an utter clod. You don't want to talk about—"

"No, I don't mind." Indeed, she'd been wishing all along that he were here to talk to. "The last time I saw Jamie was eleven years ago in the visiting room at the Plymouth House of Corrections. After that, he . . . well, he seems to have deliberately avoided me. He was probably sick of me telling him what he was doing wrong with his life and how to fix it—especially since I was no paragon of clean living myself. But at least I was discreet. He was utterly reckless, insanely so. I know I must have been tiresome, but he was . . . he was just a *boy*. Fifteen years old, brought up in squalor, almost no education. He could barely read and write."

"Fifteen. That's awfully young to be thrown into a prison full of seasoned plug-uglies."

"I'm pretty sure that livery holdup—the crime that put him behind bars—was the first time he'd done anything like that. I always suspected Duncan put him up to it, or that he was doing it to impress Duncan, and of course Duncan didn't bother to discourage him. It was so sad, because he'd been such a sweet, well-meaning kid. He looked like an angel. He had the most beautiful hair, like spun gold. He'd been born with it, and it never changed. It was always overgrown. I used to have to comb it every time I saw him, but I liked combing it. I'd retie his neck scarf. I'd wet my handkerchief and clean his face."

Squeezing her hand, Will said, "It sounds as if you loved him very much."

"I always loved him. That never changed, not a bit, not even after he started getting in trouble. I loved him despite the course his life was taking, perhaps even because of it, because he was so luckless and ill-fated. For years, I've felt guilty every time I thought about him, because I've been blessed with such good fortune, whereas he . . ."

"You created your own good fortune, Nell. You endured the same nightmarish childhood as Jamie, but you rose above it, as is your nature."

Most people follow the path wherever it leads them, Cyril used to tell her. *Others hack their own way through the brush and always seem to end up on higher ground. You're of the second sort.*

She said, "Jamie may not have had much in the way of backbone, but he wasn't a bad person. He didn't deserve what happened to him."

"Of course not."

"I didn't cry at the funeral," she said. "I didn't even cry when Cyril told me he'd died. I want to, but I just can't. It's as if there's this great black storm cloud inside me, swollen with rain, but the rain just won't come."

"Is it because you hadn't seen him in so long, do you think?"

"I suppose so. It just doesn't feel real. *Jamie* doesn't even seem real anymore. He's like one of those bleary, faraway memories, where you're not sure if it really happened or you just dreamt it. I didn't even see his body. Cyril wouldn't let me, because of . . . you know. Its condition."

"He was right. You wouldn't have wanted to see your brother like that, Nell."

"No, I should have. At least then, this wouldn't be like some bad dream I just can't seem to shake off. It would be *real*. I saw Jamie's photograph when Cyril took me to speak to the chief constable, but it isn't the same."

"Give it time, Nell. Grief is a complicated thing. The last thing you need right now is to feel guilty because you're not grieving exactly the way you think you ought to be."

She turned her head to smile at him. "I've missed this, Will. You've always been so easy to talk to."

"Most people would disagree with you, I think. I'm very glad you're not one of them." He turned her hand over and stroked his thumb across her palm and wrist, sending warm shivers up her arm and into her chest. "So it's 'Cyril' now," he said quietly.

"I'm sorry?"

"Your Dr. Greaves. You call him Cyril."

"He asked me to."

"Mm." He pulled a cigarette case out of his trouser pocket and stared at it, as if trying to decide whether to give in to temptation.

"I should be going back," Nell said.

Will looked as if there was something he wanted to say, or ask, but in the end, he just stood and offered her his hand. He walked her across the lawn and onto the back porch, where he kissed her again, with great tenderness this time.

"I wish I could sleep with you," he whispered as he rubbed his cheek against hers. "Just that. Just fall asleep curled up with you between cool sheets, feeling the breeze from the bay through the window, and hearing the sound of the waves."

"It sounds like heaven."

"Good night, Nell."

"Good night."

Chapter 7

"THEY'RE out back gettin' supper started," said the big, rumpled fellow who opened the front door of Hannah Gilmartin's farmhouse-cum-boardinghouse late Monday morning. "Chicken soup with dumplings. My mouth's waterin' already."

Nell and Will followed him through the rambling old house, most walls of which were adorned with at least one crucifix or steel engraving of the Holy Mother. They passed through the kitchen, in which three men were sitting around a big pine table drinking coffee, and out the back door to the barnyard—a patch of packed earth bordered by a gnarled old oak, a peach tree heavy with fruit, a dilapidated barn, and a handful of other small outbuildings. One of them was a chicken coop, judging from the furious squawking and scrabbling emanating from within. Steam rose from a huge copper kettle hanging over a fire pit next to a crude lean-to housing clotheslines and wooden laundry racks.

"That's Mrs. G. over there." Their escort pointed across the yard to a large woman tying a length of cord to a branch of the oak, and retreated back into the house.

"Mrs. Gilmartin?" said Will as they approached her. "May we have a word with you?"

Turning, she gave them each a swift head-to-toe appraisal as she finished tying the cord, at the end of which was a little noose. She wasn't so much obese as burly, a red-faced, sweat-sheened giantess in a head scarf, darkly stained apron, and pigskin gloves. "I don't rent rooms to couples or females," she said in a deep-chested voice seasoned with a bit of a brogue. "Or Protestants."

"We're not here to rent a room, ma'am." Will

handed her his card. "I'm William Hewitt, and this is Miss Cornelia Sweeney. Miss Sweeney is the sister of James Murphy, the young man who died when your cranberry shed burned down."

"Stepsister," Nell amended, remembering Chief Bryce's puzzlement over her name.

Mrs. Gilmartin surveyed Nell's chic black walking dress, shirred bonnet, and crochet gloves as she pulled a leather knife sheath from an apron pocket. "You don't look much like the sister of a roughneck like that." Turning toward the chicken coop, she cupped her hands around her mouth and bellowed, "Claire Caitlin, what the divil's takin' you so long?"

"I'm *tryin'*," came a high-pitched, breathless voice from within the coop.

Mrs. Gilmartin raised her exasperated gaze to heaven.

Nell said, "I'm very distressed about how my brother died, as you can imagine, and I was hoping to reconstruct his final days."

"Ain't nothin' I can tell you about that Murphy fella other than I wish he'd of picked somebody else's place to hide out at—and set fire to. I can't get too het up about it, though, seein' as it was the good

Lord's work. An eye for an eye. That's what I told that Chief Bryce, and that's what I'll tell you, stepsister or no."

"Perhaps your daughter—"

"My daughter don't know nothin' about no murderin' thief."

Will bristled on Nell's behalf. Touching his arm, she said, "My brother and I followed different paths in life, but he was the only family I had left, so I'm sure you can understand why I'm curious about his death and the days that led up to it." As Mrs. Gilmartin, looking unmoved, was opening her mouth to respond, Nell said, "You know, I think I've seen you. Don't you attend early Mass at St. Catherine's?" Nell did, in fact, recognize her from church, as Father Donnelly had said she would; Hannah Gilmartin was a hard woman to miss.

Mrs. Gilmartin blinked in surprise, her expression softening. She slid a bone-handled hunting knife from the sheath, produced a whetstone, and set about sharpening the blade. "Yeah, I reckon you mighta seen me at St. Cat's. Hunh. I took you for one of them lace curtain lasses of the Orange persuasion 'cause of the way you're flashed up. Sorry for the insult, miss."

Will looked down and rubbed his chin to hide his smile. He was as pale as ever, with an indolent heaviness to his eyes that served as a constant reminder to Nell of his seemingly inextinguishable appetite for opiates.

She'd lain awake for hours last night contemplating the evolution of her relationship with Will over the past two and a half years, culminating in Saturday night's bittersweet reunion in the boathouse. She'd finally fallen asleep around two in the morning, only to awaken sweating and shaking from a dream that the house was burning down around her, and there was no one to put it out but she—a bucket brigade of one. She grabbed the basin off the washstand and ran into the bathroom, but when she tried to fill it up, all that came out of the faucet was a series of long, excruciatingly slow drips. The drips gleamed in the fiery luminescence, each one striking the porcelain sink with a metallic clatter. Nell had looked closer, only to find the sink filling up steadily, inexorably, with hypodermic needles.

That morning, over the dawn breakfast on the back porch that had become Viola and Nell's summer ritual, Viola said, during a pause in the conversation, *You know, it would be quite all right with me if you were to remarry. You'll be a free woman soon, with any luck, so I thought you should feel . . . unencumbered.* Nell, quite certain that she'd been expected to remain unwed until Gracie's early adolescence, had ruminated on the matter over her eggs bourgeoise before asking Viola if she wouldn't please avoid mentioning the divorce petition to others, including Will. After several long minutes of disconcerting silence Viola said, *Do be careful in your choice of a husband, Nell. I know something of the safe and convenient marriage. I also know something of ardor. The former should be chosen over the latter only when one has exhausted every option at one's disposal. We humans are weak and needful creatures, and there is really no substitute for true passion.*

"I got her! I got her!" A wanly pretty girl in a striped apron lurched out of the chicken house gripping a screaming red hen upside down by its feet.

"Bring her here, then," said Mrs. Gilmartin as she ground the knife over the whetstone with purposeful strokes. "And keep ahold of her. If she gits loose from you now, there'll be no catchin' her a second time, you can be sure of that."

The girl stared at Nell and Will—but especially

at Nell—as she carried the writhing bird to her mother, holding it at arm's length. She was as delicate as her mother was brawny, a waifish little thing with brown hair and guileless eyes. Nell supposed she must have seen this girl at St. Catherine's in past summers, although she couldn't place her. Where she did recognize her from, Nell realized with a start, was Jamie's funeral. Claire was one of the weeping females whom Nell had taken for a heartbroken admirer of her brother.

"This here's the sister of that fella that burned up in the cranberry shed," Mrs. Gilmartin told Claire, gesturing toward Nell with a knife. "I told her we don't know nothin' 'cept what we told the constables."

Nell said, "Claire, didn't I see you two weeks ago at my bro—"

"Maybe in town," she said with a furtive little shake of her head. "Maybe at the market."

"Get that bird trussed up," her mother told her, "before she gets away from you."

Claire looped the noose around the chicken's feet and pulled it snug, all the while standing as far from the thrashing creature as she could.

"Get the pail," her mother told her, "and this time

don't tarry. You got to do it fast when the time comes."

The girl lifted a dented tin pail from the ground and held it under the hen, averting her gaze and squeezing her eyes shut.

Mrs. Gilmartin seized the hen by its beak, stretched its neck, and sliced off its head. The bird let out a screech; so did Claire.

"The pail!" her mother yelled as blood sprayed from the flapping, headless chicken, spattering her and her daughter both. Nell and Will backed up hastily; it was fortunate that they were both dressed entirely in black.

Claire thrust the pail up over the bird, holding it there until it had ceased twitching, which didn't take long. She set it on the ground directly under the limp hen to catch the remaining dribbles of blood.

"I said *fast*." Mrs. Gilmartin threw the chicken head at Claire, who sidestepped it with a squeal.

"Sorry, Ma." Claire was, indeed, a "young" nineteen, as Cyril had said, with her high, thready voice and timid manner. She wore her hair in two braids; a silver crucifix hung around her neck.

"I understand you got trapped in the burning cranberry shed trying to help my brother," Nell told

Claire. "You risked your life for him. I'm grateful for that."

Mrs. Gilmartin, crouching down to clean the blood off her knife by stabbing it into the dirt, let out a disapproving grunt.

"Where *is* the cranberry shed?" Will asked, looking around at the outbuildings, none of which appeared to have been exposed to fire.

Gesturing toward a patch of woods to the south, Claire said, "It's off thataway, between the cranberry bogs and Mill Pond Road."

"Had you known he was hiding out in there before the fire?" Will asked.

"Of course she didn't," said Mrs. Gilmartin as she straightened up, pulling off her gloves and stuffing them in her apron pockets. "What kind of a question is that? Claire, fetch me a peck basket from the barn, the one with the swing handle."

As Claire ran off to do her mother's bidding, Will said, "I'm just asking because it sounds as if that shed is pretty isolated. I was wondering what she was doing there."

"The harvest starts soon," said Mrs. Gilmartin as she untied the apron and slung it over her big shoulder. "It's Claire's job to clean up the shed and get it ready, 'cause we use it for storage and whatnot the rest of the year. See, that's where the berries are taken after they're picked. We pack 'em in bushel boxes to cure—or my workers do, the fellas I hire at harvesttime. After about a week or ten days, they're sorted and barreled and sent off to market."

"When did you start cleaning the shed?" Nell asked Claire as the girl returned from the barn and handed the basket to her mother.

"It's a big job, so I start around the middle of July."

"Most years," said Mrs. Gilmartin, shooting a look at her daughter. The older woman plucked a peach from the tree and sniffed at it. "But this year, she kept putting it off, one excuse after another. That's how come we didn't know Murphy was there till the night of the thirty-first, when it burned down."

"You were cleaning it at night?" Nell asked Claire.

"I got other chores to do during the day. So I headed down there after supper, and when I started getting close, I smelled smoke, and I heard him— your brother—I heard him scream, so I ran and I seen the shed was on fire. I guess I thought I should do somethin', so I—"

"He screamed for help?" Nell asked. "He actually said, 'Help me'?"

"Well, yeah," she said, seeming a little thrown by the question. "Anyways, that's how I knew he was in there."

"Was he still screaming after you got inside the shed?" Nell asked.

"What? No. No, he wasn't makin' any noise at all. I think maybe he was already . . . you know."

"Could you see him?" Will asked.

Claire stared at him for a moment, then looked away, as if considering the question. "Um, no. I don't think so, no. He must've been behind something. There's all this stuff in there, or was—crates and barrels, a table, the cranberry sorter . . . All of it was on fire, and there was so much smoke I couldn't hardly see. Anyways, come to find out my skirt's on fire and some bushel boxes stacked up near the door had started burning and fell over, so I couldn't get out that way."

"What did you do?" Will asked.

"I grabbed a shovel and smashed a window and crawled out that way, and then I ran back to the house fast as my feet could take me, screamin' till my throat was raw. The boarders come runnin' out with a bunch of them gallon buckets the cranberry pickers use. One of them got on a horse and went to fetch Ma, and we all—"

"You weren't home?" Nell asked her mother.

Adding another peach to her nearly full basket, Mrs. Gilmartin said, "I was on my way to St. Cat's to bring some chicken fritters to Father Donnelly. I'd made extra just for him. I only got about half a mile down the road before George came riding up to tell me what happened. By the time we got back, the fire was almost out. But the cranberry shed can't be saved, just the sorter, 'cause it's metal. The shed'll have to be torn down."

"How do you think the fire started?" Will asked her.

"I reckon Murphy got careless with a match. Maybe he got drunk and fell asleep with a lit cigarette. Or maybe he knocked over a candle."

"Did you happen to notice any strangers on the property around that time?" Nell asked.

"Only folks on the property were my boarders and the fellas I hire to tend the bogs, and they been workin' for me for years. Wouldn't none of them set fire to my cranberry shed. Why would they?" Jogging the basket up and down as if testing its weight, she said, "I got to bring these to Father Donnelly. He's expecting me by noon. So if you folks don't have no more questions . . ."

"Do you mind if we take a look at the cranberry shed?" Nell asked.

"Can't see the point of it, but help yourselves. Just follow that path," she said, pointing. "It'll take you south through them woods. You'll pass the bogs on your right, next to the pond, then the path splits off in two directions. You want to keep to the left, headin' east. There's another little patch of woods, and then you'll come upon what's left of the cranberry shed."

Will said, "May I ask why it's so far from everything else?"

"That's to make it easier to get the cranberries to market once they're cured and sorted. If you was to keep following that path through the woods, you'd come right out onto Mill Pond Road."

"I appreciate you letting us see it," Nell said.

"Ain't much to see, but you'll find that out for yourselves. Claire, I expect you to get busy plucking and dressing that bird. It better be in the pot by the time I get home."

As Mrs. Gilmartin was walking away, Claire

turned to Nell and said softly, "I'm sorry about your brother, Miss Sweeney. But I'm glad he got laid to rest in the churchyard, by a priest. He got buried proper, so he's with Jesus now."

"I hope so," said Nell, reflecting on Claire's theological naïveté in believing that a lifetime of sin could be negated by the simple expediency of a Christian burial. She declined to mention that she had applied just that morning to have her brother's body unearthed from that very churchyard. "Claire, I wonder if you would help us find our way to the cranberry shed."

"But . . ." Looking toward the dead chicken, she said, "Ma wants me to—"

"We won't keep you," Nell said as she curled an arm around the girl's shoulders and started down the path that led to the cranberry shed. "But I *would* like to chat with you a bit."

"What about?"

"About my brother's funeral, for one thing. Your mother doesn't know you went to it?"

"Oh, Ma would have a conniption if she knew. She said he was a godless hoodlum, and that he got what was coming to him. You won't tell her I was there, will you, miss?"

"Of course not. But I am curious as to why you went, given that he was a total stranger to you, and a criminal, at that, one who was responsible for burning down your cranberry shed."

Claire looked down, her hands buried in her apron pockets, and jerked her birdlike shoulders. She walked that way in silence as the path entered the woods. "I kind of felt . . . I dunno. Like a person ought to have someone there when he's laid to rest, even someone that didn't know him."

"But you did know him, didn't you?" said Nell, seeing Will, out of the corner of her eye, give her a look of surprise. "He wasn't a stranger to you at all."

Claire looked at her sharply as she stopped walking. "I . . . I'm sure I don't know what you—"

"Your mother told you I was Jamie's sister, but she never told you my name. Yet you called me Miss Sweeney. You knew my brother was hiding out in the shed, Claire. You talked to him. You befriended him. He talked about me."

"Ma said she'd whip me to the bone if I told anyone."

"But you didn't tell," Will pointed out. "The clever Miss Sweeney sorted it out on her own."

"I'm not trying to get you in trouble," Nell told

her. "I'm just trying to piece together my brother's last days. If you could help me to do that, I would be very grateful. And I promise your mother won't find out what you've told me." Curling her arm around Claire's, she continued on down the path through the woods, Will following behind. "How long did you know that Jamie was hiding out on your property?"

"He told me that was what you and his ma used to call him—Jamie. I called him Jim, on account of that's what he told me his name was—Jim Murphy."

Duncan had been the first one to call him Jim, Nell recalled. He'd said "Jamie" made him seem like a little boy.

Rephrasing the question Claire had neglected to answer—she seemed a bit mentally unfocused—Nell said, "When did you realize Jamie was living in the cranberry shed?"

"It was the first time I went down there to start cleaning it up."

"Which wouldn't have been the evening of Sunday the thirty-first, as you told us," Nell said, "but sometime before that."

"It was the Saturday before, and it was in the afternoon. I mean, not Saturday the *day* before, but—"

"Eight days before," Nell said. "That would've been July twenty-third. Four days after . . ." *Murdered Susannah Cunningham of Boston, aged 37 yrs.*

Nell squinted from a sudden onslaught of sunlight as the path emerged from the woods to continue along the eastern edge of a field next to Mill Pond. The field had been planted with four rectangular cranberry beds of about an acre each— carpets of low green vines speckled with ripening berries. Between each bog, and extending to the path on which they walked, were makeshift roadways of wooden planks. The path, which widened as it passed the bogs, was rutted with years' worth of close-set wheel tracks, probably from wheelbarrows used to transport the harvested berries to the cranberry shed.

Will said, "So you'd gone to the cranberry shed that afternoon to start setting it right, and you found James Murphy there. That must have been quite a shock."

"I screamed, but couldn't nobody hear me way out there. He stood in front of the door so I couldn't get out, and he told me to calm down, talkin' real soft and slow. He said he didn't mean to do me no harm. I didn't believe him at first. I never been so scared in my life."

"Did you know who he was?" Nell asked.

"He asked me that. I told him I figured he was one of them fellas they'd been looking for, the ones that killed that lady. He told me it wasn't him that done it. But he said the cops didn't know that, and they'd hang him if they caught him."

Nell's relief at hearing this was tempered by the knowledge that Jamie might have just been saying that to get Claire on his good side.

"He seen my crucifix," Claire continued, "so he said he knew I was a God-fearing girl and would do the right thing. And then I remembered I'd seen him once or twice at St. Cat's, and I thought if he went to Mass, he couldn't be all bad. He pulled his Sacred Heart medal out from under his shirt and said it meant more to him than anything. He said his ma gave it to him before she passed."

"She did," Nell said. *This is the Sacred Heart of Jesus, Jamie. Wear it for strength. You're my only son. You're the head of the family now. Make me proud.* Nell was gratified, if a bit surprised, that her brother had kept the medal all these years. "Claire, I don't suppose you would know what became of that medal. It wasn't among the items that were taken off my brother after the fire."

Claire regarded Nell blankly for a moment, then looked away, shaking her head. "I couldn't say, miss. Sorry."

"So Jamie earned your trust?" Will said.

"He swore on his ma's soul that he didn't kill that lady and he wouldn't hurt me. I could see in his eyes he was tellin' the truth. He had these eyes, they were . . . like the eyes of Jesus in the pictures. You couldn't look away from 'em." She bit her lip, her eyes damp.

"I know," Nell said. As, no doubt, had Jamie, who'd always found it indecently easy to bend females to his will. He'd been thirteen the first time he talked himself under a girl's skirts; she was seventeen, a voluptuous redheaded barmaid.

"He said he could tell I was kind and sweet and would help him," Claire continued. "He said I was beautiful, not just on the outside like some girls, but deep in my heart, where only God could see. I think I musta turned red as a beet."

"Because he said you were beautiful on the outside?" Nell asked.

"No fella ever told me that before."

"So you helped him," Will said. "The next day when everyone else was at that ice cream social, you came back and gathered up some food and whatnot and brought it to him."

"I went back there every day after supper to bring him food, stuff I didn't think Ma would miss. She thought I was going there to clean up. I knew I couldn't let her know Jim was there, 'cause if she knew, she'd turn him in for sure. She's real big on walkin' the straight and narrow." Claire seemed to be warming to her subject, perhaps because she'd had no one to confide in until now.

"Jim used to ask me to stay and talk," she said, "'cause he was lonely. Nobody ever talked to me like he did, all quiet and serious. He talked about important things. He made me feel important. He asked me what I thought about this or that. It got to where all I could think about during the day while I was doing my chores was gettin' back to the cranberry shed that night, so I could be with Jim. He always seemed so happy to see me. But then he'd get . . ."

"What?" Nell said. "Melancholy? Did he feel guilty about Mrs. Cunningham?"

"No, no not at all. I told you, he said the other fella

done it, a fella called Davey. Jim said he was real mad at Davey for doing that. And that's why they went their separate ways, 'cause Jim didn't want to have nothin' more to do with Davey after that."

"My brother didn't feel bad at all that an innocent woman died during a burglary he had engineered?"

Claire frowned as if trying to remember. "No, he told me it was all Davey's fault, and his conscience was clean."

They came to the split in the path that Mrs. Gilmartin had mentioned and followed the left-hand fork as it veered into another patch of woods. Nell thought about the tears Jamie used to shed as a boy when one of the orphaned or injured animals he would try to rescue didn't make it. She recalled his frenzied sobbing whenever someone died—not just family members, but neighbors he barely knew, or other inmates of the poor house. It would appear that his skin had thickened since she'd last seen him, perhaps as a result of his years behind bars.

"How did your mother find out he was hiding in the cranberry shed?" Will asked the girl.

Claire winced. "She came there one night to see

how much I'd gotten done, and she saw me and Jim . . . We was . . ." She bit her lip, her cheeks stained pink.

"Oh," Nell said. "Claire, don't be embarrassed. You're not the first young girl to be seduced by a handsome, charming—"

"What? No, I didn't mean that. We weren't . . . you know. Jim said he knew I was a good girl, so he didn't want to . . . you know, compromise me. But he . . . he kissed me sometimes, and I kissed him back, even though he said he couldn't ever . . . pay me his addresses or nothin'. He said I'd best know up front he was gonna be leavin' soon as the time was right, and that would be the end of us. I asked him was he gonna say good-bye or would I just come out there one night and find him gone. He said he was sick of good-byes. He'd had a whole life-time of good-byes."

"Yes, he did," Nell said in a low shaky voice. His father, his mother, his siblings, one after the other, Duncan, her . . .

Will stroked her shoulder.

"The day Ma came to the cranberry shed," Claire said, "Jim and me was laying together on this quilt I'd brung him to sleep on, and I know what Ma was thinking, but it wasn't like that. We were just kissing, but she didn't believe it. She started ranting and railing and threatening Jamie 'cause she knew right away who he was, 'cause of him living there in secret. He just stood there real calm, while she screamed in his face. She slapped him—hard—and he just took it like it didn't even happen, even though she's as strong as a man. He told her he was sorry for livin' on her property without permission, but she should know I hadn't done nothin' sinful. She called him a liar and slapped him again. I couldn't stop crying. She said she didn't want to turn him in 'cause then everybody would find out I gave myself cheap to a murdering thug, but that she would unless he left that night."

"When was this?" Nell asked.

"A couple-three days before the fire. Thursday, I think."

"But he didn't leave?" Will asked.

"He told her he would, but . . ." Her voice damp and unsteady, Claire said, "I wish he had. I wish he'd of just left like he should of, gotten off the Cape and gone somewhere far away."

Nell patted her arm, saying, "So do I."

"I told Ma he left," Claire said.

"And she didn't check to make sure that was true?" Nell asked.

"Um, no. No, I guess not."

"And then, three nights later," Will said, "you went there to see him, only to find the shed on fire and Jamie trapped inside."

No wonder Claire had risked her life to save Jamie's, Nell thought. She had clearly been smitten by him.

"We're close," Will said. "I can smell it."

Nell inhaled the smoky tang of burned wood.

"That's it," said Claire, pointing to a clearing up ahead where the path widened into a road big enough to accommodate the wagons used to transport the cranberry barrels to market. To the left of the road was the roofless, carbonized vestige of a structure about the size of the hovel in which Nell and Jamie had spent their early years.

They entered this blackened skeleton through what was left of the doorway. Burned-up rafters, roofing shingles, barrels, lath pallets, crates, chairs, tables, and tools lay amid drifts of ash and cinders. In the middle of the room stood a freestanding contraption of blackened metal with a large chute that looked as if it had been cobbled together from old farm equipment—the cranberry sorter, presumably. To one side of it lay a folded quilt burned around the edges, but not down the middle, where Jamie had slept—and died.

Will noticed the direction of Nell's gaze and rested a hand on the small of her back. He said, "Why don't you go wait in the buggy? I'll have a look around here."

"No, I want to see it. At least it's something, something *real*, something I can touch."

"When the constables came to take the body away," Will asked Claire, "did they search through this stuff at all?"

"I wasn't here, but Ma said they just put the body in a hearse and left."

"I'm surprised there's even this much left," said Will, gesturing toward the charred remnants of the walls. "It must have been burning for some time before you raised the alarm, considering how long it would have taken you to run back to the house."

"There's a shortcut through the woods that takes about half a minute," she said from the doorway. "Less than that if you're running, and I was running fast as I could. I didn't want to take you that way 'cause you're dressed so fine, and there's no real path. If you don't mind my asking, what are you folks looking for?"

"I want to know whether Jamie died of the fire or the smoke," said Nell as she knelt to stroke a hand over the quilt bedding, which was damp from yesterday's rain. It wasn't the truth, of course, for she and Will were primarily looking for evidence, such as blood or a knife, that Jamie may have died from being stabbed in the chest. Unfortunately, the top quilt was of a honeycomb pattern in shades of brown, maroon, and black that had suffered a month's worth of summer rainstorms. The dye—and any blood that may have been there—had run together in mottled splotches clustered mostly in the middle, where the weight of Jamie's body had created an indentation. She noticed scorched remnants of a brown woolen blanket, bits of which Cyril had seen on Jamie's corpse.

"He apparently died flat on his back with a blanket over him," Nell said.

Claire said, "He musta been sleeping."

"But you heard him scream for help."

"Oh. Um. Yeah." The girl looked down, jamming her hands in her pockets. "I reckon that wasn't exactly true."

Nell said, "You made that up to explain why you would have gone running into a burning building that was presumably unoccupied."

Claire nodded. "It wouldn't of made no sense 'less I thought somebody was trapped in there. Course I did figure Jim was in there, but I couldn't of told Ma that, 'cause I already told her he left."

"Claire, how do *you* think this fire started?" Will asked as he lifted a fallen beam and tossed it aside.

She shrugged. "I reckon it was like Ma said, a cigarette or a candle."

"Did you ever see him smoke?" asked Nell as she lifted her skirts to pick her way through the wreckage, looking for a knife blade.

"No, uh-uh." She thought about it for a moment. "But maybe he just didn't smoke in front of me. Gentlemen ain't supposed to smoke in front of ladies."

"Well, yes," Nell said. Except that Jamie hadn't exactly been what one would call a gentleman. As she recalled from her days among the petty grafters and hoods of Cape Cod, the men had never let the presence of a female keep them from enjoying their cigarettes.

Nell said, "There was no match safe among his personal items, and I don't see any here. They're always metal, so if there was one, it would have survived the fire. I'll keep on the lookout for melted wax that might have been a candle, but I haven't seen any yet. As for your mother's theory that he was drunk, there's no flask or bottle around, at least not in this general vicinity."

After a few more minutes of picking and searching among the detritus, Will said, "Look at this." He made his way over to Nell, rubbing the ash off two pale pink shards of glass, one small and the other about the size of his hand.

"A bottle?" Nell asked.

"I don't think so," he said, showing her his finds. The pieces of glass were curved and embossed with a design of swags and medallions. "I found them some distance apart. I think they're from a lamp."

Nell took one of the shards and held it to her nose, inhaling a hint of camphor. In concert with the acrid old smoke odor filling her nostrils, it made her stomach roil. She closed her eyes and took a deep breath, but that only made her feel as if the ground were shifting beneath her feet.

"Nell?" Will grabbed her by the upper arms. "What's the matter? You're white as a—"

"It's nothing. It's the smell."

"Here, put your head down," he said, supporting her with his arms around her waist.

It helped. After a minute, she told him she was better and he helped her straighten up. With a sardonic little smile, he said, "You've become rather delicate since I last saw you."

You have no idea.

"You all right, miss?" Claire asked. "There's a little stream nearby if you want some water. I'd bring you some if I had a cup, but—"

"Thank you, but I'm fine, really," said Nell, wanting to deflect attention from her "delicate" condition. Nell asked Claire if she had any camphene lamps on the property. The most common fuel for lamps until the advent of kerosene about ten years ago, camphene was a volatile mixture of alcohol and turpentine with a little camphor to mask the turpentine smell.

Claire frowned in evident puzzlement. "Camphene?"

"Burning fluid," Will said as he continued sorting through the wreckage.

"Oh. Um . . . I dunno. Yeah, I guess maybe there's a couple old ones in the barn. Ma doesn't want 'em in the house anymore."

"Was one of them pink?" Nell asked.

"I reckon."

"Here's the burner," said Will, holding up what looked like a blackened brass jar lid with two splayed spouts for the wicks, each dangling a brass cap by a tiny chain. "It looks as if an oil lamp was converted into a camphene lamp by replacing a regular burner with a camphene burner. Not an uncommon practice a few years ago, but not a safe one."

"Camphene produces gases that can explode if they get too hot," Nell explained to Claire. "The more camphene in the lamp, the bigger the explosion."

"Did you hear an explosion as you were approaching the shed that night?" Will asked her.

"Um, no. I, um, I don't think so."

"If you were some distance away, it may have just sounded like a pop."

"I don't know. Maybe."

Will said, "I'll wager if we checked the barn, we'd find one of those lamps missing."

"Or did *you* bring it here?" Nell asked her.

"No!" Claire said, holding her hands up. "I never brought it. *He* must of."

Nell said, "If you did, I can understand your feeling a certain measure of guilt, given that this lamp probably started the fire. But you shouldn't. You were only trying to—"

"I didn't bring it!" she said, her face reddening. "I *didn't*."

"All right," Nell said. "I'm sorry. I didn't mean to upset you."

"It's just . . . this whole business has been so . . . so . . ." Claire lifted her apron to wipe away the tears welling in her eyes. Will handed her his handkerchief, which she accepted with a bashful nod. "I'd best be gettin' back to that chicken," she said. "Ma won't like it if she comes home and doesn't find it in that pot."

Nell stopped Claire with a hand on her arm as she turned to leave. "My brother . . . He told you about me?"

"Oh, yes, miss," said Claire as she wiped her ruddy nose with the handkerchief. "He called you Nelly. He told me all about how you and him and your little sister, the one that died . . ."

"Tess," Nell said in a near whisper.

"He told me about the poor house, and how he left and fell in with a bad crowd. He told me you was always at him to straighten up, but he didn't listen."

"I nagged him about how he should live his life," Nell said. "He grew to resent me. Eventually he just didn't want to have anything more to do with me."

"That ain't what he told *me*, miss. He said you were the only person in the world that ever really cared about him. He said you tried to talk sense to him, but he thought he was smarter than you, only he really wasn't. He said after he got sent to jail the first time, he didn't want you to see him no more till he got out of there and set himself straight."

"He wanted to go straight?"

"That was his plan, 'cause he was ashamed of himself, ashamed of what you thought of him. He said you sent him a letter in jail telling him your husband done you wrong, and that made him feel worse than ever. He said you never would of fell in with that fella if it weren't for him. When he got out of jail, the war had just started, so he went straight to Boston and enlisted."

"But you had to be eighteen to enlist," Nell said. "Jamie would have been just seventeen."

"He fibbed about his age. He just wanted to do somethin' right for once to prove to you that he wasn't just some low-life grabber. After he mustered out—I think he said that was June of 'sixty-four—he came back here and tried to get honest work, but it was hard to come by even with so many fellas still off fighting. I reckon he was telling the truth, 'cause Ma says things ain't what they used to be 'round here. She says all the young fellas are leavin' the Cape 'cause there ain't enough jobs to go around."

"That's true," Nell said. The industries that had supported the Cape for so many years—whaling, fishing, shipping, the saltworks—had been in decline for the better part of a decade.

Claire said, "Jim didn't want to get sucked back into his old life, but he did, 'cause it was the only way to put food in his belly."

Will said, "It seems to me he could have gotten work in Boston or New York."

"He told me the Cape was his home," Claire said. "He felt lost in Boston, like he was a little ant crawling along the sidewalk trying not to get stepped on. But here he had friends, even if they was the wrong kind of friends, and he knew the lay of the land. But a couple times, he told me he wished his folks would of stayed in County Donegal instead of comin' here for a better life, 'cause it wasn't no better life. He said he would of rather been a fisherman in the old country, no matter how poor, than what he was."

"Did he say whether he'd ever tried to contact me?" Nell asked.

Claire shook her head. "He heard you were a governess in Boston, and he said he was real proud of you, but that you wouldn't be proud of him if you knew he was right back where he'd always been. He said he missed you something terrible, but he just couldn't let you see him like that."

"Oh." Nell's voice sounded small and faraway to her ears.

Wrapping an arm around her waist, Will said softly, "Come, Nell. There's nothing more to see here."

Nell nodded forlornly.

"Um, before you go," Claire said, "I . . . I lied to you. I'm real sorry." Fumbling under the collar of her calico frock, she withdrew a little silver pendant on a chain. "He, um . . . he gave me this."

The oval disk depicted a heart crowned with flames and encircled by thorns—Jamie's Sacred Heart medal, the one her mother had presented to him on her deathbed. "He *gave* it to you?"

"Right after my ma lit into him and stormed off. He said it was the only nice thing he had, and he wanted to thank me for bringing him all that food and being so good to him. He said I come along just when he needed a friend. I told him I couldn't take it, but he said he wanted me to have it. I was afraid if I told you about it, you'd want it back. And it's . . . it's all I've got left of him. But that was selfish and wrong, 'cause you're his sister, and it belonged to your ma, and you should have it."

Claire reached behind her neck to unhook the chain, but Nell stilled her hand. "Keep it."

"Oh no, miss, I couldn't."

"You were there when he needed someone," Nell said. "I wasn't. Please keep it. My mother would have wanted you to have it."

Chapter 8

T HAT night, when Nell came downstairs after tucking Gracie into bed, Cyril Greaves was standing at the foot of the stairs holding a *Barnstable Patriot* extra with a headline in two-inch letters.

DAVID QUINN CAPTURED.

Second *Bloodthirsty Burglar* Under Arrest.

Evaded Justice for 34 Days.

A Wave of Relief Washes Over Cape Cod.

"They caught him this afternoon," said Cyril as Nell skimmed the extra, which described how Quinn had grown a beard to disguise himself before seeking work as a deckhand on a codfish trawler. Nevertheless, the captain had recognized him from his pictures in the newspaper articles and summoned the Falmouth constabulary. He said it was Quinn's "lunatic bug-eyes" that gave him away.

"I want to talk to him," Nell said.

"To find out whether it was he or your brother who shot Mrs. Cunningham?"

"That, and whether he knew that Jamie was hiding out in that cranberry shed." Nell told Cyril what she and Will had found out during their visit to the Gilmartins' farm that morning—Claire's having known that Jamie was there all along, her mother's ensuing rage, the shattered camphene lamp—and what they hadn't found, namely any sign of blood or a knife blade.

Cyril said, "If you must talk to Quinn, you'll have to do it in the morning. They've got him in a holding cell at the Falmouth Police Station, but they'll be transporting him to the Plymouth House of Corrections tomorrow afternoon. I don't want you going alone, though, not to talk to a character like that. I can't go with you, because I have appointments all morning."

"I'm sure Will won't mind coming with me."

"Where is he?" asked Cyril, glancing around.

"In the boathouse, I assume. I haven't seen him since before supper. He won't eat with us when Mr. Hewitt is here."

"Let's go talk to him."

"Now?" Nell thought about the morphine and hypodermic apparatus on the dressing table of Will's bedroom. If Cyril were to see that, there would be no way to convince him that Will was anything other than a confirmed degenerate.

"Humor me," he said, offering his arm. "I've always wanted to see the inside of that boathouse."

"HE must not be in there," said Nell with relief as Cyril knocked on the door of the guest suite for the third time. "He's probably out on the dock."

"Aren't there stairs to the dock from the veranda?"

Cyril asked as he opened the door, gesturing Nell ahead of him. "Let's take those."

Nell's suspicion that this was just a ruse to get a peek inside the famous Hewitt boathouse was confirmed when Cyril lingered in the sitting room to look around. She took advantage of his preoccupation to make a beeline for the bedroom with the intention of hiding the tray before he could see it, but all she found on the dressing table were the most recent issues of *The Lancet* and the *New England Journal of Medicine*. She conducted a swift survey of the bedroom, then checked the adjacent bathroom—nothing.

Cyril called out, "Nell, look at this."

Oh, no. She returned to the sitting room with a sense of dread, only to find Cyril standing over the desk in the corner holding a sheet of writing paper inked in a neat, sharply angled hand.

"Before you revile me for reading someone else's correspondence," he said, "ask yourself if you could have resisted doing so if you'd noticed this." He pointed to the words engraved in the upper-right-hand corner of the writing paper in Gothic lettering: 𝔈𝔵𝔢𝔠𝔲𝔱𝔦𝔟𝔢 𝔐𝔞𝔫𝔰𝔦𝔬𝔫.

Nell snatched the letter out of his hand and read it.

Washington, August 12th, 1870.—

My dear Will,

I write this in the fervent hope that it will find you well on the way to recovery from the bayonet wound you suffered during the Battle of Wissembourg. From Marshal MacMahon's account to Ambassador Washburne, which the ambassador was kind enough to share with me, it is clear that you exhibited courage much beyond the call of duty in risking your life to save those two wounded French soldiers. This came as little surprise to me, given the extraordinary valor you exhibited at the Battle of Olustee during the War Between the States, as attested to by your commanding officers.

In grateful, if belated, acknowledgment of that fearless service in defense of the Union, it is my privilege to grant you this nation's highest award for bravery, the Medal of Honor. Were it not for the mistaken inclusion of your name on the Andersonville death rolls back in '64, the process of selecting you as a recipient would have concluded long ere this. My secretary will contact you with the particulars as to the ceremony,

*which can take place either here in Washington,
or when I visit Boston in October.*

*I look forward to reminiscing with you over a
bottle of whiskey—and to saluting you with the
most heartfelt respect and admiration when I
present you with the Medal of Honor.*

*Yours very truly,
U. S. Grant*

"This is incredible," Nell said.

"He's turning it down."

"What?"

Cyril lifted from the desk a sheet of heavy vel-
lum embossed FALCONWOOD, on which Will had
begun penning his reply, and handed it to her.

August 22, 1870
President Ulysses S. Grant, Washington, D.C.

Dear Mr. President,

*Humbled though I am to be considered for
such an honor, it is one I feel unworthy to accept. My actions on the field of battle were no
more remarkable than those of many other men,*

soldiers and surgeons alike, some of whom paid
for their valor with their lives. It is with regret
but deep gratitude that I must

Nell reread the half-finished letter, shaking her head. "This is so like Will." She looked up to find that Cyril had wandered off. Turning, she saw him standing in the kitchen doorway holding the tray of morphine paraphernalia.

"This was on the kitchen table," he said.

Nell closed her eyes.

"You knew about this." It wasn't a question.

Before Nell could summon a response, there came footsteps rising from the stairs that led to the boat slips beneath them.

Will appeared in the entrance to the stairwell, stark naked and dripping. His gaze shifted from Nell, with the letter in her hand, to Cyril holding the tray. "Find everything all right?" he drawled.

Nell gaped, as did Cyril, not because of Will's state of undress, but because of his right forearm, which was slashed open from elbow to wrist. The gash was deep, ragged, and purulent, the surrounding flesh hotly inflamed. In comparison, the puckered, long-healed bullet wound on his right thigh, which had shocked Nell the first time she saw it, seemed a mere scratch.

"Will—*my God*," Nell said.

Cyril set the morphine tray on the desk and crossed to Will, scrutinizing the wound with his trenchant physician's gaze. "How long has it been exhibiting sepsis?"

"I've got it under control." Will grabbed a towel off the back of a chair and scrubbed it over his chest.

"You've got the *pain* under control," said Cyril, nodding toward the cluster of needle marks and bruises on the upper part of his right arm. "But the injury itself . . . well, quite apart from its severity, it's badly putrefactive. Are you running a fever?"

Will averted his gaze from Cyril's as he dried off. His hesitation was telling. No wonder he was so pale and glassy-eyed. It wasn't just morphine intoxication. His body was struggling—with limited success, it would seem—to fend off the infection ravaging his arm.

"I'm getting my medical kit." Cyril turned to leave.

"I'm dealing with it—I told you," Will said, but Cyril ignored him as he left the suite and sprinted down the stone staircase. "Greaves. *Greaves*!" Will muttered something under his breath as he wrapped the towel around his hips.

Nell crossed to him and stroked his damp forehead, which was hot to the touch. "For God's sake, Will. Why on earth did you tell us it was just a minor wound?"

He took her hand, pressed it to his cheek, and leaned into it. "I didn't want you to fret over me, but now that you are, I rather like it."

"The morphine—I knew you were taking it again, but I didn't realize it was for pain. I thought . . ."

"You thought I was slipping back into old habits. Can't say as I blame you. I haven't exactly proven myself a model of sobriety."

Will kissed her palm and retreated into the bedroom, leaving the door open. "Best to put something on before the good doctor returns," he said, pulling a pair of linen drawers out of a clothespress and stepping into them. "It's no easy task to project an air of authority when one is stark naked. Curious that Greaves didn't raise any objection to it, considering your presence."

"He was focused on your arm."

Will smiled as if at a prevaricating child. "He knows you've seen me naked. You told him about us."

She sighed and nodded.

He attached a pair of narrow black suspenders onto trousers of the same color, shook them out, and pulled them on. "Do you think that was wise?"

"I trust him absolutely," she said, feeling a pinch of guilt that Cyril knew even more about them than did Will; he knew she was going to have his baby.

Shrugging into a starched white shirt, Will said, without looking at her, "Seems a rather intimate subject for a conversation with a man you haven't seen in what—six years?"

"We're old friends, Will."

"You're old lovers."

Nell's face stung with heat right up to her hairline. "It's not . . . W-we're not . . ."

"Oh, Nell." He came to her, took her face in his hands, and kissed her. "Of course you're not. But you were at one time, and . . . well, it's always been something of an abstraction to me, you and he having been together that way. But now that I've met him, it all seems just a bit too real. Don't misunderstand," he added, holding her at arm's length so that he could look her in the eye. "I don't judge. God, how could I, considering my own past? This isn't about condemnation, it's about the knot in my chest every time he says something intelligent or does something thoughtful or displays one of his many other estimable qualities, which seems to be every bloody second of every bloody day."

"Wait," she said through a chuckle. "You're put out because he's a good, decent man?"

"If only he were a braggart," Will said as he buttoned his shirt, "or a prig, or had a lisp, or perhaps a hump. Yes, that would do nicely. I'd settle for a hump."

Hearing Cyril's footsteps on the stairs outside, Nell said, "Why won't you let him treat your arm?"

"Because I don't need him. I'm a doctor, remember? I treated thousands of limbs injured just as badly as this one during the war."

By cutting them off, one after another, to the screams and sobs of the other wounded men waiting for their turn under the bone saw, because it was the only way to deal with such grievous wounds in the field. *Nine minutes per leg,* he'd once told her. *That's all it took me.*

"Let's do this in the kitchen," Cyril said as he strode through the room with his medical bag—the same cracked old leather satchel he'd used when she'd assisted him in his rounds. "The light's better in there."

"I told you," Will said. "I've got it under—"

"What you've got," Cyril said, turning in the kitchen doorway to face Will, "is an arm that will have to be amputated above the elbow if you ignore it much longer."

"That's what he's afraid of," Nell said. "That's why he doesn't want you to treat him, because he thinks you'll want to cut it off."

Will glowered at her. She glowered back.

"You do realize it's a vicious circle," Cyril told him as he disappeared into the kitchen. "In an effort to stave off amputation, you avoid medical care, which only worsens your condition, increasing the likelihood that you'll lose the arm."

Will looked as if he were trying to summon a refutation, but having no luck. He raised his right arm to rake the wet hair out of his eyes, winced, and used the left. The hair fell right back down again.

"That's the first time I've seen you exhibit any pain," Nell said.

"I'm due for more of that." He cocked his head toward the morphine. Nell was familiar enough with the drug, from her nursing experience and Will's use of it, to know that doses low enough to keep one alert and functioning could dull the pain but not eliminate it. She realized Will's arm must hurt constantly, especially when he used it in a normal fashion, but he'd been stiffening his backbone and carrying on as if nothing were amiss. Nell didn't know whether to find that admirable or idiotic.

"What I want to know," Cyril said, raising his voice to be heard from the kitchen, "is how you could have allowed the infection to progress to the point of necrosis. You're a physician. You must have known what was happening."

Approaching only as far as the kitchen doorway, Will said, with a disgusted sigh, "It was that bloody mail packet. It was a floating cesspool. I'd brought along a bottle of carbolic for cleaning and dressing the wound, but it fell and broke during rough seas our second day out. I was left with nothing but morphine for the pain and seawater as an antiseptic. It does help a little—that's why I go out in the bay every evening to soak the arm, that and because it's soothing—but it's a poor substitute for carbolic. The arm was a cursed mess by the time I disembarked in Boston."

"Nell, do you think you could put a pot of water

on to boil?" Cyril asked as he washed his hands at the sink. "The biggest one you can find. And see if there are any Epsom salts in the cupboard."

"Epsom salts?" she asked. "You're not going to purge him, are you?"

"No. Oh, and we could use some clean napkins or towels or the like."

Will stepped aside for Nell, who started pulling out drawers, amused that Cyril had reverted so automatically to their old doctor-nurse relationship.

Producing a roll of gauzy bandaging from his medical bag, Cyril said to Will, "I assume you *have* been using carbolic since you got back."

"Of course, full strength. But—"

"*Full strength?* That stuff is corrosive at full strength. It can even be toxic."

"It did cause some burning of the surrounding tissues, but I felt that was better than losing the arm altogether. I'm beginning to think it's not quite the magic wand Lister claims, though, because it doesn't seem to have done much good."

"The infection must be so deep-seated at this point that the carbolic just isn't reaching all of it. And, too, pure carbolic can actually impede the healing process. Ah, just the thing," Cyril said as

Nell handed him the box of Epsom salts she'd found under the sink.

"Surely you're not proposing that I use *that* in place of the carbolic."

"You're to use it in place of the seawater. Make a strong, hot solution of it three times a day and soak your arm for an hour at a time. This," he said, holding up a little jar of crystalline powder, "is your substitute for the carbolic."

Coming closer so that he could read the label, Will said dubiously, "Lunar caustic? You're going to cure me with *silver*?"

"Silver nitrate," Cyril said. "About a year ago, I came across an article about the inability of aspergillus niger to grow in silver vessels. I recalled our cook, when I was young, dropping silver coins into a jug of milk to keep it fresh when it couldn't be kept in the icebox. So I started using a solution of silver nitrate on open wounds, and so far I haven't seen a single one go bad."

"Will these do?" asked Nell, setting a stack of tea towels on the table.

"Quite nicely. If you wouldn't mind washing your hands, I could use your assistance." To Will he said, "Our first priority is gaining access to the deeper infection, and to do that, I'm going to have to lance the wound where necessary, clean it out, and cut away the necrotic tissue. After that, we'll soak it in the Epsom solution, then pack it with gauze soaked in silver nitrate. The silver will leave an indelible black stain on the wound and surrounding flesh, but over time, as new skin grows in to replace the old, it will disappear."

He untied a leather roll and whipped it open on the table with a steely clatter, revealing a gleaming array of scalpels, bistouries, lancets, forceps, and scissors.

Will regarded the instruments in silence for a weighty moment. He looked oddly young and vulnerable in that untucked shirt and dangling suspenders, his hair drying in wavy tendrils over his forehead.

Cyril pulled a chair out from the table and gestured to it.

With a capitulatory sigh, Will took a seat and rolled up his right sleeve.

Cyril retrieved a little brown vial and a hypodermic kit. Screwing a needle onto the brass syringe, he asked Will how much morphine he could tolerate without diminished respiration. "You'll want your maximum safe dose for this."

With a fleeting glance at Nell, Will said, "I'll do without, thank you."

"She already knows you're a hero, old man. The president himself has vouched for you." Shaking the brown vial, Cyril said, "How much?"

"Really, I'd much prefer to keep my wits about—"

"Will, please," Nell quietly implored. "Don't make me watch you suffer."

He looked from Nell to Cyril, then sat back, letting out a long, grudging sigh. "Thirty milligrams."

Cyril prepared the solution and filled the syringe.

"I'll do it," said Will, reaching for it.

Before he'd even finished giving himself the injection, his eyes grew bleary, his body slumping bonelessly in the chair. He withdrew the needle and went to lay the syringe on the table, but it slipped from his hand and fell to the floor.

"Right, then," said Cyril. "Let's get to work."

Chapter 9

"DON'T see why not," Chief Bryce told Nell and Will the next morning when they asked to see David Quinn, but as he led them upstairs to the second floor, he warned them that they wouldn't find the prisoner very talkative. "He's always been a real chaw-mouth, the kind that'll yak a blue streak just to hear himself talk, but now he's got this greenhorn public lawyer, Edwin Thursby, who's making him keep his mouth shut. Kid's with him right now, trying to hash out a defense. Quinn pled not guilty at his arraignment, claims he's an innocent man, says he was out fishing while Susannah Cunningham was getting shot."

"Alone?" Nell asked.

With a roll of the eyes, Bryce said, "They're always alone."

"Will?" Nell said as he paused at the top of the stairs to lean against the wall, eyes closed. "Are you—"

"I'm fine," he said, a claim belied by his waxy complexion, the rigid set of his jaw, the tremor in his hands.

"He sick?" Bryce asked.

"He's not contagious," Nell said as she stroked his shoulder. He was, in fact, suffering both from his throbbing arm and from morphine withdrawal, for he had adamantly refused, since last night, to take any more. Nell had assured him there was no shame in using it as an anesthetic, but there'd been no reasoning with him. She'd told him she was perfectly capable of driving to Falmouth alone, that he should stay put and rest; he wouldn't hear of it. She knew he was trying to prove something to her, which only exacerbated the guilt she already felt for having kept him in the dark about the divorce petition and pregnancy.

It reassured her considerably, of course, to know that he'd been using the morphine not for inebriation, but for pain relief—this time. But would there be other times? Would there be more lapses into opium smoking, more trips to Shanghai, more gambling? As far as she knew, he still had no intention of returning to Harvard, nor of disclosing to Gracie that he was her father.

She wanted to tell him everything. She *ached* to tell him. But then what?

"If you don't mind my asking," said Bryce as he led them through a warren of corridors, "what do you expect to gain from talking to Quinn? If you're hoping he'll admit it was him that fired the fatal shot, and not your brother, I gotta tell you, you're in for a disappointment. He's been real tight-lipped. We haven't been able to get a peep outa him."

"I *would* like to exonerate my brother of murder, if only posthumously," she said, "but I'd also like to find out if Quinn is responsible for his death."

Bryce paused, frowning, with his hand on a doorknob. "Your brother burned to death."

"We have reason to believe he may have taken a knife to the chest," she said. "We'll have a better idea tomorrow if that's actually what he died from.

We've just come from the town hall. Our application to exhume my brother's body has been approved. The exhumation will take place tomorrow morning, and Dr. Hewitt and Dr. Greaves will perform an autopsy in the afternoon."

"He *had* an autopsy," Bryce said.

"A *real* autopsy," replied Will, speaking for the first time since he'd been introduced to the constable.

Bryce swung the door open with a smirk. "Suit yourself, but if you ask me, it's a waste of time and effort. Visitors!" he announced as he waved Nell and Will into the room ahead of him.

It was a small, windowless meeting room with a hulking constable standing guard over a table stacked with papers, at which sat two men. One was a pink-cheeked fellow in a high collar with well-oiled, crisply parted hair: the lawyer, Edwin Thursby.

The other man was slight and dark, a demonic elf with a sparse moustache and bulging eyes. He wore a black coat with drooping shoulders and a collarless shirt buttoned up to the throat. In one of his manacled hands he held a half-smoked cigarette. This was David Quinn.

Thursby rose to his feet with a quizzical expression as Nell entered the room. Quinn surveyed her up and down, his mouth parting to reveal a jumble of yellowish teeth.

"David." The young attorney nudged his client, who kept his gaze fixed on Nell as he stood. Quinn slid his tongue over his teeth as he lifted the cigarette to his mouth.

"This here's the stepsister of your dead pal," Bryce told Quinn as he leaned against the wall, arms crossed. "She wants to know if it was you or Murphy that shot that lady, and if you stuck a knife in Murphy's chest."

So much for the subtle approach, Nell thought.

Apparently dissatisfied with that dismal excuse for an introduction, Will said, "The lady is Miss Cornelia Sweeney. I am Dr. William Hewitt. You will put that out, Mr. Quinn."

Thursby, belatedly registering the breach of etiquette, plucked the offending cigarette from his client's hand and stubbed it out in a yellow soup plate overflowing with butts, earning him a poisonous glare from Quinn.

Bowing to Nell, the young lawyer said, "I'm sincerely sorry for your loss, Miss Sweeney. However, I'm sure you can understand that I can't allow my client to engage in a conversation of this nature. I must therefore ask you and Dr. Hewitt to—"

"Allow?" Quinn spun on Thursby with eye-popping indignation. In an odd, nasal voice, he said, "You're my mouthpiece, Thursby, not my ma. You don't tell me what to do. You got that?"

Seating himself as he tugged Quinn down onto his chair, Thursby leaned in close and said, in a low voice, "I'm your attorney, David. I'm here to guide and represent you. Given the circumstances of this case, it just isn't smart to be talking to—"

"You sayin' I'm stupid?" Quinn was quivering all over, as if he were on the verge of detonation. "You sayin' I'm some jughead that needs to be told what he can do and what he can't?"

"No, of course not. But—"

"I'm the boss. You work for *me*." Quinn stabbed his thumbs into his chest. "And if I wanna talk to the lady, I'm gonna talk to the lady. You got it?"

Thursby turned away with a resigned sigh.

Quinn turned his greasy grin on Nell and gestured with his bound hands toward the chair opposite his. "Miss, uh, Sweeney, is it?"

"For the record," said Thursby as Nell and Will seated themselves, "Mr. Quinn could not have shot

Mrs. Cunningham, as he was fishing in Eel Pond at the time. And as for your brother, it is my understanding he died of—"

"I never known Jim had a stepsister," Quinn said as he lounged back in his chair, his gaze crawling over Nell. "'Specially such a tasty little bit of—"

"Be careful, Quinn," Will said in a low, even voice. "I've never taken my fists to someone in manacles, but I find myself in the mood to break with tradition this morning."

"Dr. Hewitt," Thursby said, "if you're going to threaten my client, I shall have to ask you to leave. This situation is trying enough for Mr. Quinn. He's an innocent man who's being persecuted simply because he was acquainted with James Murphy. The assumption that he was Mr. Murphy's partner in this heinous crime has arisen from guilt by association."

Will said, "Yes, well, according to Claire Gil—"

"Dear me, I had no idea," Nell interrupted. Pitching her voice high and soft, she said to Quinn, "You're going through all this just because you and my brother were friends? That's dreadful! If Jamie were alive, I know he'd have something to say about that."

"Yeah, I reckon he would, at that," Quinn said.

Sitting forward with a conspiratorial little smile, Nell said, "You know, Mr. Quinn, I really wouldn't mind it one little bit if you smoked. I don't think it's rude at all. In fact, I've always found cigarettes rather dashing. Some people think they're low class, but I think they impart a certain . . . virile sophistication."

From the corner of her eye, she saw Will cast a jaundiced look at the ceiling. He was cradling his right arm with his left, she noticed.

"That's swell of you," Quinn said, sneering at Thursby as he fumbled in his coat for a hand-rolled cigarette and a match. "Real swell."

"They told me you were a fugitive for weeks," Nell continued. "I must say, it was pretty savvy of you, knowing you'd be connected with my brother— but how absolutely *horrid*, having to hide from the police when one has done nothing wrong."

"I was hounded day and night," Quinn said through a flutter of smoke, "but not by the cops. They tacked up my picture, but nobody pays them things any mind, not in my neck of the woods, anyway. It was the husband, Cunningham. He tried to run me to ground in my own neighborhood, got all my friends lookin' to put a bullet in me—or them I thought was my friends. Come to find there wasn't no safe place for me to hole up, and nobody I could trust. I had to keep on the move, keep my head down every second of the day, sleep with one eye open."

"Yes, I saw the handbill Mr. Cunningham distributed," Nell said, choosing her words with care because of the intensity with which Quinn's earnest young lawyer was following the conversation. "It was vigilante justice, nothing more. But of course it isn't justice at all when an innocent man ends up arrested for a crime he didn't commit."

"It wasn't just them handbills," Quinn said. "He was on my scent—Jim's, too—long before he started handin' them out. He was like a bloodhound, askin' folks if they seen us, tellin' 'em they could make an easy five grand if they popped us . . ."

"David." Thursby closed a hand over Quinn's shoulder. "You'd best—"

"When did he start nosing around like this?" Nell asked Quinn.

"Oh, he'd been gunnin' for us since we done the job." Quinn stilled in the act of raising the cigarette to his mouth.

Thursby closed his eyes.

Will smiled at Nell in a way that said, *Touché, Cornelia.*

Quinn stabbed out the cigarette. "Shit."

Bryce pushed off the wall with a whoop of triumph. "That sounded like a confession to me."

"It was nothing of the sort," Thursby said. "It was an innocent statement, open to interpretation."

"Yeah, well, I got a pretty good idea how a jury's gonna interpret it," Bryce said.

"Did you shoot Susannah Cunningham?" Will asked Quinn.

Thursby said, "David, don't—"

"No, uh-uh," said Quinn, shaking his head. "Nope. I sure didn't. That was Jim."

"Really?" Nell said.

"I didn't even bring a gun. I don't even own one." Quinn drew on the cigarette, his gaze darting this way and that—everywhere but at Nell. "It was Jim that had the jumpy trigger finger, not me."

"Well, that's very sobering," Nell said. "And surprising. Jamie was always an abysmal shot, never could get the hang of it. Of course, I hadn't seen him in over a decade. It's possible he practiced and got better. Still . . ." She turned to Chief Bryce.

"Didn't you say Mrs. Cunningham was shot directly in the middle of the forehead?"

"Yep. You'd of thought it was blank range, but it had to be a good thirty, forty feet, given the size of that library—and dark, to boot."

"That sounds like the work of an expert marksman," Nell said, "someone with unerring skill and cool nerves, a real deadeye. That kind of accuracy with a gun . . ." She lowered her voice to a throatier timbre and pressed a hand to her throat, as if on the verge of swooning. "I've watched sharpshooters practicing with targets. It's breathtaking to see a man exhibit such mastery over his weapon. My heart races just watching him load and cock it, but when he squeezes the trigger and that bullet penetrates the bull's-eye . . ." She hitched in a breath. "I shiver just thinking about it."

Every man in the room was staring in dazed silence at Nell. Will's mouth curved into a smile. Young Thursby's ears were a deep, scalding red.

Quinn whispered something into his lawyer's ear, but sound traveled in that little room. ". . . get away without hangin' if I didn't—"

"It doesn't matter who actually shot her," Thursby whispered back. "It's felony murder either way—but you don't want to be admitting to any more than you—"

"I did it," Quinn told Nell, his bulbous eyes glittering with pride. "I shot her. Jim didn't even have a gun, he didn't like 'em. It was me."

"For pity's sake, David," Thursby groaned.

"We didn't think no one was home till she come traipsin' downstairs, callin' out"—he adopted a falsetto—"'Freddie? Is that you?' I drop that cabinet full of boat crap we're draggin', whip out my Remington, and *bam*!" Quinn formed the shape of a gun by clasping his hands and extending a forefinger, which he pressed to the center of his forehead. "Neat as a drill, right through the braincase." He aimed the finger at his mouth and mimed blowing into the barrel.

Thursby was sitting back in his chair, looking defeated.

Quinn lit another cigarette. "Jim, he was on the high ropes after that, screamin' and hollerin', sayin' why'd I have to shoot her—me sayin' she shouldn't of snuck up on us like that. He threw a punch at me, but I dodged it and he lost his footing and landed on his ass. Didn't get up, just hung his head and started boo-hooin' like a schoolgirl."

"He cried?" Nell said.

"A grown man, for Chrissakes. I didn't know whether to laugh or puke. See, he knew the lady from working on her gardens, 'cause he'd be tillin' and she'd be plantin', and they'd get to talkin'. He said she used to bring him lemonade with ice in it and slices of lemon, and sometimes cherries, and it was the best lemonade he ever drunk. He said he used to say funny things 'cause he liked the way she laughed, with her whole face kinda crunchin' up, which I never could picture. You ask me, he was sweet on her, never mind her bein' older and a rich married lady. Anyways, me and him parted ways after that. He said he had his fill of me, didn't ever want to lay eyes on me again, called me some names he didn't ought to call me. I said good riddance."

Will said, "Was that the last time you saw him?"

Quinn blew a plume of smoke in Will's direction. "I told you—we parted ways. That means I never seen him again."

"Are you sure?" Nell asked. "You didn't start worrying that he'd get caught and pin the killing on you? At the time, you thought only the actual shooter would get charged with murder. You wanted to make sure he couldn't testify against you, so you snooped around and discovered he was hiding in the Gilmartins' cranberry shed. You sneaked in there with a knife one night while he was sleeping and—"

"Knives are for bitches," Quinn said.

His hands curling into fists, Will said, "Don't give me an excuse, Quinn."

"That's not an answer," Nell said. "Did you stab him or not?"

"No, I did not." He was looking right at her.

"Did Mr. Cunningham arrange for you and Jamie to steal that nautical collection?" she asked.

His eyebrows quirked. "How'd you know that?"

That question seemed to echo in the expressions of every man there, including Will.

She said, "When I first spoke to Chief Bryce about this case, he told me that Mr. Cunningham's handbills offering a reward for your death were printed up the day after Jamie's body was identified, which would have been August first. Prior to that, nobody even suspected Jamie—nor you, Mr. Quinn. But a few minutes ago, you told me that Mr. Cunningham had been 'gunning for you since you did the job,' which was July nineteenth. So, for two weeks, Frederick Cunningham had known exactly who broke into his home that night."

"Hunh," said Chief Bryce, who, had he the slightest aptitude for police work, would have sorted this out with no help from Nell.

"There are only two ways Mr. Cunningham could have known this," Nell said. "One possibility is that he figured it out through his amateur sleuthing. Then, rather than tell the police, he decided to exact personal revenge against his wife's murderers by having them killed. The other possibility is that he contracted with you and Jamie to steal that collection while he and his wife were both away. You've just confirmed for me that it was the latter."

"Why the hell—'scuse me," Bryce said. "Why the heck would he want his own property stolen? 'Specially something so valuable?"

"For the insurance money?" Will suggested.

Quinn nodded as he took a puff. "That, and Jamie was supposed to fork over half of whatever he made fencin' the stuff. It was Jamie he cooked up the deal with. He figured Jamie was a drifter who'd jump at the chance to make a haul like that, and he was right. Jamie said he felt bad, though, 'cause Susannah—that's what he called her, not to her face, but to me—he said she'd talked about that collection, said it meant a lot to her. She told him her husband was always on her to let him sell it, 'cause they had money troubles, but she told him he should sell his sailboat instead—only he wasn't about to do that. So that's why he had to go around her back and set it up to look like a burglary. Jamie hated to go along with it, but he wanted that money. He said he could maybe buy himself a fishing boat and earn an honest living. He was always talkin' about that—gettin' outa the life."

Will met Nell's gaze. She just shook her head.

"Cunningham told Jamie where to find the spare key," continued Quinn, who, unrestrained by his now apathetic lawyer, was industriously "yakking a blue streak." "He said to bring a wagon and a partner, and to do it on the nineteenth, when he'd be in New York and the missus on Martha's Vineyard."

"Only he wasn't counting on the ferry being canceled because of that storm over the Sound," Bryce said.

"That's 'cause he's an amateur," Quinn offered helpfully. "He wasn't thinkin' about what-all could go wrong. He was just thinkin' about the money."

Bryce said, "For what it's worth, he seemed pretty broken up when he got off that train."

"Guilt will have that effect," Will said. "His wife never would have died if he hadn't conspired to have that collection stolen."

"He was grief-stricken," Nell said, "but he was scared, too. He knew that if Jamie and Quinn were caught, they'd most likely spill the beans about his little scheme, and then *he'd* end up behind bars, too."

"So he tried to silence them before they could be arrested," Bryce said.

"He may have even succeeded, at least as regards my brother," Nell said. "If Jamie really did die from a knife wound, I'll wager the killer is five thousand dollars richer."

"So Cunningham's guilty of . . . let's see." Counting off on his fingers, Bryce said, "Conspiracy to commit murder, attempted insurance fraud, obstruction of justice . . . And who knows what the D.A. will charge him with for trying to steal and fence his own property."

"It's the conspiracy to commit murder that I'm interested in," Nell said. "I want to know how and why my brother died."

"Quinn's arrest is Cunningham's worst nightmare," Will said. "Does he know about it?"

"Sure," Bryce said. "I sent one of the boys over

to his place yesterday evening to tell him. Now I'm gonna have to head over there myself and arrest the sorry gump."

"Assuming he hasn't flown the coop one step ahead of you," Will said.

"If he hasn't," Quinn said as he lit another cigarette, "he's not just an amateur, he's a horse's ass."

CHIEF Bryce, flanked by two of his men, pounded on the front door of Frederick Cunningham's Falmouth Heights summer house—a palatial white mansion right on the Sound—while Nell and Will waited on the badly overgrown front lawn.

Bryce had objected when Nell asked to come along so as to question Cunningham about Jamie's death, saying it was highly irregular to bring a civilian along when making an arrest, especially a female civilian. He'd relented when Will had asked him if he thought the *Barnstable Patriot* might be interested in running a story on the governess who'd gotten to the root of the Cunningham case by outdetecting Falmouth's chief constable.

Bryce tried the door; no luck. They circled the

house, but the back door was locked as well. It was a glass door, so Nell could see into the huge, sumptuously appointed library and through its column-flanked doorway to a hall lined with marble statues. There was an odd stillness to the house, right down to the dust hovering in shafts of sunlight from the windows on the west wall. On the east wall, next to a fireplace with an ornately carved overmantel, was an empty space with four tamped-down marks on the Aubusson carpet where heavy cabinet legs had stood.

They checked the carriage house, whose three bays held an elegant landau, a park phaeton, and a utilitarian wagon. The upstairs servants' quarters were unoccupied—beds stripped, dressers empty.

"I say, may we help you?" a man called out as they were heading toward the nearby stable. They turned to find an aristocratically handsome middle-aged couple in bathing attire and sunglasses walking toward them from the adjacent backyard.

Bryce introduced himself to the neighbors, who identified themselves as Alice and Walter Wyndham, and asked them if they knew of Frederick Cunningham's whereabouts.

"I haven't seen him since last night," Mr. Wyndham said. "He came over to give me his boat."

"His sailboat?" Nell asked incredulously.

He nodded. "The *Oh, Susannah.* I know, it was his prized possession. I was dumbfounded. He said he knew I'd always admired it, and he wouldn't be able to use it anymore, so he signed the title over to me. I confess I was at a complete loss."

Will said, "Did he explain why he wouldn't be able to use it?"

"I asked him, but he didn't answer, simply ignored the question altogether. Most peculiar."

"We think perhaps it just reminded him too much of *her*," said his wife. "Ghastly business. Poor Freddie hasn't been the same since. He's been living there all alone, you know, fending for himself—sent the staff back to Boston weeks ago. He's been paying the Livingstons' stableman to care for his horses."

"What time did he come over to give you the boat?" Nell asked Mr. Wyndham.

"Well, let's see . . . It was while the sun was setting. I remember, it was a particularly exquisite sunset, and I remarked on it, but Cunningham ignored that as well."

"The sun's been setting around seven o'clock," Will said.

"When did your man come by to tell Cunningham about Quinn's arrest?" Will asked Bryce.

"It was at the end of his shift, so a little after five."

"And you didn't see Mr. Cunningham at all after he signed over the boat?" Nell asked the couple.

"Well, I *saw* him," said Mrs. Wyndham. "Just from a distance, but—"

"When was that?" Bryce asked.

"I believe it was around nine o'clock, perhaps a little later. Night had fallen, but there was still that lovely violet glow to the sky. I'd been embroidering a pillowcase upstairs in my sitting room, but it started to feel stuffy, so I went out onto the veranda." Pointing to her house, she said, "It faces the Sound, as you can see. After a few minutes, I saw Freddie come out of his house and walk down to the beach. It was dark, of course, so I couldn't make him out very well, but I did see him swim out into the Sound."

"He went *swimming*?" her husband said.

"Is that surprising?" Bryce asked.

"He doesn't care for it," Mrs. Wyndham explained. "Susannah loved it, but Freddie says he prefers to have a boat between himself and the water at all times."

Her husband said, "He admitted to me once, after a few whiskeys, that he's terrified of being in water too deep to stand in, because he's such a poor swimmer. He's always afraid he'll end up too far from shore and not have the strength to get back."

"Did you see him return from his swim last night?" Will asked Mrs. Wyndham.

"No, I'd gone inside to work on the pillowcase."

Silence fell over the group. Nell turned to gaze out over the Sound, as did the others. It looked like one of those postcards promoting Cape Cod, an idealized summer seascape executed in translucent washes of azure and aquamarine, with a scattering of puffball clouds overhead.

Chief Bryce said, "I'll send a boat out, but they won't find anything, not yet." With a ponderous sigh, he added, "It usually take a while."

Chapter 10

NELL, sitting in the gloomy, brocade-swagged front parlor of Packer's Mortuary the next afternoon, heard footsteps on the stairs from the basement "Cold Room," where Jamie's disinterred body had been delivered about two hours before. She looked up from *The Innocents Abroad*, which she'd been halfheartedly reading, to see Will enter the room from the hallway, straightening his coat.

"You're done?" she asked as he came to sit next to her on the green velvet couch.

He nodded. "Sorry to make you wait so long, but we wanted to be thorough. Greaves will be up in a few minutes. He's sewing up the incisions and dressing your brother for reburial tomorrow."

He took her hand, and she was gratified to find his own hand, if not entirely steady, at least less palsied than it had been yesterday. His color was better, and he didn't seem quite as strained, which she hoped was an indication that his pain was lessening, along with symptoms of morphine withdrawal. He swore he been following Cyril's Epsom salts and silver nitrate protocol religiously, and that the wound was already looking better.

"Did you find the nick on the left fourth rib?" Nell asked.

"We did. It was almost certainly made by a very sharp blade. Also, the third rib opposite the nick is cracked, which is consistent with a large knife being plunged into the chest with great force. The nick looked fresh to me, and in fact when we removed the chest plate, we discovered a deep laceration through the pericardial sac into the heart. And there wasn't the slightest trace of soot in the bronchi, so we know for sure he wasn't breathing when the fire started."

Sitting upright, Nell said, "Then he *did* die from a knife wound."

"He did, indeed—but not on July thirty-first, when the cranberry shed burned down. He was killed about three days earlier."

"Three days? How can you know that?"

Will hesitated a moment before saying, "We found charred larvae on the body. Do you recall me describing the life cycle of blowflies?"

She did. It had been two years ago, as they'd stood in a field over the grisly, maggot-infested remains of Bridie Sullivan. A sudden wave of nausea seized Nell as she visualized her brother's mouth and eyes and nose crawling with those loathsome things. She took a deep breath, but it didn't help. Yanking her hand from Will's, she sprinted to the washroom.

Will called her name. She locked the door, dropped to her knees before the W.C., and retched violently.

"Nell!" Will banged on the door, twisted the knob. "What's wrong? Let me in."

To see me like this? She grabbed the sink and hauled herself to her feet. *Not bloody likely, Dr. Hewitt.*

"I'm fine. I'll be right out." She rinsed her face and mouth, adjusted her shirred bonnet, and rejoined him.

Will apologized for having brought up the subject of the larvae as he escorted her back to the parlor, an arm curled protectively around her. "You'd never shown a weak stomach before, so I thought . . . But that was foolish. It's different when it's your own brother. I should have realized—"

"You should have been frank with me, as you were," she said as they sat back down on the velvet couch. "You couldn't have known I'd have that kind of reaction. I, er, I assume the larval stage indicated that they'd hatched about three days before the fire."

"That's my best guess, given typical summer temperatures in this area."

"If he'd been dead for three days, how did the fire start?" Nell asked. "We've been assuming that pink lamp exploded, but if Jamie wasn't alive to have lit it . . . I mean, a camphene lamp, even a full one, couldn't have burned for three days straight."

"No, it would have to have been lit sometime after Jamie's death." Will sighed. "The more we learn, the more questions arise."

"The most important question on my mind right

now is, where was Claire Gilmartin when my brother was lying there dead in that shed? She told us she went to see him every day."

He said, "We can pay the Gilmartins a visit on our way home, if you'd like."

"I would."

Will looked down, nodding. "I, er . . ." He pulled a folded handkerchief out of his coat pocket and handed it to her. "I thought perhaps you might like to have this."

Nell looked at it, bewildered. It was just a handkerchief, far too light in weight to be wrapped around something, yet he said, "Open it."

She set it on her lap, the white linen a stark contrast to her black silk skirt, and unfolded it. Lying in the center of it was a tuft of gold thread tied with string. She lifted it carefully and held it in the light of the gas sconce on the wall above.

It wasn't thread.

Her heart clenched, sucking a gasp from her.

Oh, God. She stroked the silken blond strands with a fingertip, remembering the way her comb used to slide right through them, Jamie rolling his eyes impatiently at first, then smiling that drowsy little-boy smile, saying, "Don't stop, Nelly."

The memory melted behind a trembling sheen of tears as Nell closed her fist around the lock of hair. Grief punched her in the stomach, squeezing the air from her lungs. She curled up with a hand over her mouth, her back shaking in silent agony.

"Nell." Will wrapped her in his arms, tucking her snugly into his embrace. "Oh, Nell, I'm sorry. I'm sorry."

She sucked in a breath to tell him he'd done nothing wrong, quite the contrary, only to erupt in helpless, wrenching sobs. Will untied her bonnet and pulled it away. He cupped her head in his big hand, pressing her tear-dampened face to his chest. Nell wept convulsively, as if her body were straining to expel not just the pain of Jamie's final, desperate days, but the entire dark and bitter past to which he'd been her last remaining link.

Will kissed her head, saying, "I'm an imbecile. Don't cry, sweetheart. I didn't mean to upset you. I love you."

Nell grew very still, her breath coming in sharp little hitches as she strove to get herself in hand. *I love you.*

He rubbed his cheek against her hair, saying, "I didn't mean to say that. You're not free to hear it, and God knows your situation is difficult enough without me complicating things. But I'm selfish and I'm weak, and I love you so much, and it's been so excruciating not being able to—" His voice snagged. "Forget I said it."

A floorboard squeaked. Nell craned her head to see Cyril Greaves standing in the doorway. He turned and left. A moment later, there came the sound of the front door opening and closing.

NELL stepped out onto the front stoop of the mortuary after a detour to the washroom to splash cold water on her face, replace her bonnet, and pull on her gloves. She paused upon seeing Will and Cyril standing near Cyril's coupé at the curb, deep in conversation.

It was Cyril who was talking, hat in hand, his expression so earnest and sober that she wished she could hear what he was saying. Will, his face shadowed by the brim of his hat, stood in that hip-shot way of his, arms folded, head down.

Cyril said something that made Will look up. Presently he lowered his head again, rubbing his jaw.

When Cyril's gaze lit on Nell, he said something

to Will, who glanced at her and then away. Cyril spoke for a moment longer, Will nodding in response.

The men shook hands. Cyril turned as he replaced his hat and gave Nell one of those quiet, enigmatic smiles of which she'd once been so fond. He raised his hand in a farewell gesture, climbed up into his vehicle, and drove away.

"IS your daughter at home?" Nell asked Hannah Gilmartin, standing at her kitchen table cutting up a slab of gristly beef with a cleaver.

"More questions?" Scowling as she hacked, Mrs. Gilmartin said, "You'll pardon me fer sayin' so, but sometimes you just gotta let the dead lie."

"I just want to thank her again for trying to save my brother's life," Nell lied. "I keep thinking about the courage that took."

"Foolishness, more like. She's an addlepated nit if ever there was one." Gathering up a handful of beef cubes in both gigantean hands, she dumped them into an iron pot next to the cutting board. "You just want to thank her? That's all? 'Cause she's got the wash to boil. She drags her feet as it is. If she gets to jawin' with you, she'll never finish up."

"We won't take much of her time," Nell said.

Slamming the cleaver into the cutting board, Mrs. Gilmartin turned toward the back door. "Come on, then."

Stilling her with a hand on her arm, Will said, "Don't trouble yourself, ma'am. You have things to do."

Mrs. Gilmartin looked from Will to Nell and back again, shifting her bulldog jaw. She looked as if she wanted to argue with him, but she finally just sighed and said, "She's out back. Don't keep her."

They found Claire standing over the big copper kettle, stirring its contents—sheets, it looked like— with both fists wrapped around a long washing stick, her slender arms quivering with the effort. Her braids were limp; sweat dripped from her red-flushed face. This was brutal work for a warm afternoon.

"You all right, Miss Sweeney?" asked the girl as she wiped her face with her sleeve. "You look like you been cryin'."

Will answered for Nell as he rested a hand on her back. "It's painful, losing a brother."

It was painful, yes, but a good deal less painful now than it had been before this afternoon. Being able to touch a part of Jamie—part of his actual, physical self—had made him, and consequently his death, much more real. Nell's explosion of grief had been cathartic, leaving her drained—it had been all she could do to sit up straight in the buggy—and yet at ease, as if all were finally right with the world. When one's brother dies, one ought to be able to mourn him so as to move on afterward. Nell hadn't been able to do that until Will had thought to snip that lock of hair.

She'd thanked him for that gift as they drove here from Falmouth, correcting his assumption that, because of her reaction, he'd somehow erred in giving it to her. She had not, however, mentioned what he'd said to her, his declaration of love. It didn't seem like the kind of conversation one should have in a coal box buggy jostling over dirt roads. Nor had she asked about that little tête-à-tête between himself and Cyril, which was clearly meant to be private—but that didn't mean she didn't wonder about it, especially given how oddly pensive Will had been ever since. He hadn't tried to make conversation during the drive, so neither had she.

Instead, Nell had closed her eyes and watched her thoughts coalesce into lazily shifting images, as often happened when she was drowsy. Sunlight flashing between the passing trees flickered red through her eyelids, casting those images into a luminous if leisurely kaleidoscope: glass bursting sharp and pink . . . the Sacred Heart of Jesus pouring blood as flames crackled all around it . . . headless chickens thrashing and screaming . . . Frederick Cunningham swimming into violet-stained oblivion . . . and Jamie grinning carelessly as he waved to her from the deck of a forty-foot sloop with *Oh, Susannah* painted across the bow. *What do you think, Nelly?* he called out as he sailed off toward the horizon. *I traded my Sacred Heart for it. I didn't need it no more, and Freddie don't need the boat.* She'd awakened with a start to Will stroking her cheek and telling her they'd arrived at the Gilmartins'.

Will nodded toward the house, drawing Nell's attention to the kitchen window, through which Hannah Gilmartin was openly peering. She abruptly averted her gaze when she saw them looking in her direction.

"Your mother doesn't seem to like the idea of us talking to you," Nell told Claire.

Lowering her voice, although Mrs. Gilmartin

was much too far away to hear them, Claire said, "I reckon she don't want me telling you about . . . you know. What I told you the other day. Me knowing about Jim being in the cranberry shed."

Nell said, "I've been thinking about the Sacred Heart medal he gave you. You realize it had to be his most treasured possession."

Will glanced at her as if wondering where she was headed with this.

Claire touched her chest over the medal that lay beneath her damp plaid shirtwaist. "You want it back?" There was a plaintiff note in her voice.

"Oh, no," Nell said. "But . . . when did you say he gave it to you?"

Looking a bit mystified by the question, Claire said, "It was the night she lit into him and told him he had to leave."

"He told her he *would* leave, didn't he?" Nell asked.

"Yeah, and then Ma went away, and that's when he gave me the medal, for bein' so nice to him."

"Yet he was still there three days later, when the cranberry shed burned down," Nell said.

Returning to her stirring, Claire said, "Like I said, he didn't leave."

Will took the wash stick from her, saying, "Allow me."

Claire gaped at him, as if astounded that a gentleman would take on such a task.

"Did your mother know that Jamie remained in the shed after he told her he would leave?" Will asked.

"What? No. It was like I said before, I told her he did leave."

"She didn't go there later that night to check and make sure?" Will asked. "Or perhaps the next morning?"

"No," Claire said, shaking her head. "Uh-uh. No. She didn't have no more to do with him, I swear. Why are you asking me this?"

Nell said, "Claire, we know Jamie didn't die during that fire."

Eyes wide, she stammered, "I—I don't know what—"

Will said, "I'm a physician, Claire. I autopsied him this morning."

"What's that? Au—autop . . ." Claire asked.

"An autopsy? It's an operation a surgeon performs on someone who's died to sort out the cause of death."

"You couldn't have done that to Jamie," Claire said in a tone of someone who was accusing someone else of lying. "He's buried in the churchyard at St. Cat's."

"We had him dug up," Nell said gently.

Claire's jaw dropped; she took a step back. "*You dug him up?* That's—that's sacrilege. It's got to be."

"God wouldn't object to us trying to find out the truth," Nell said. "We're going to rebury him tomorrow."

"Where he was before? With Father Donnelly speaking over him, all proper?"

"I can ask Father Donnelly to say a few words," Nell said.

Claire seemed to relax. "He had a Christian burial, and that means he's with Jesus. I just . . . I just don't want it undone, 'cause I don't know what'll happen to him then."

"To his immortal soul, you mean? Claire, a person doesn't go to Hell just because he's not buried in a churchyard by a priest."

"But he does. Or Purgatory. The Bible says so."

Trying to word this in a way that Claire could understand, Nell said, "The Bible doesn't actually say anything about it, but the church fathers say that people who've committed certain sins and haven't repented, or who've died unbaptized, can't be buried in consecrated ground. But that's no prediction of their eternal destiny—where their souls will go after they die. A Christian burial is an honor, a mark of respect. It has no power in and of itself to send a soul to Heaven. God is merciful. He understands human weakness. He's forgiving, especially if we recognize our sins and seek forgiveness. He mostly wants us to be good at heart. If Jamie deserves to go to Heaven, he'll go to Heaven no matter where he's buried."

"Are you sure?" Claire asked.

"Absolutely."

"I thought . . . I . . . I was so worried about him, about his immortal soul. But if all you need is to be good inside, I know he'll go to Heaven. He was sorry for what he done, breaking into that house and all."

"Because Susannah Cunningham ended up dead?" Nell asked. That would confirm what David Quinn had told them about Jamie "boo-hooing" over her murder.

Shoving her hands in her apron pockets, as she did when she was nervous, Claire said, "It . . . it wasn't really true what I said the other day about him not caring. He didn't kill her—Davey did—but Jim said it was his fault 'cause he brought Davey along. He said he hadn't pulled any jobs—that's how he put it, 'pullin' jobs'—since he got out of jail in January. Said he was tryin' to fly straight, like when he was in the Army, but it was hard to live on what he was makin' doing gardening and cutting fish and the like. He said he got greedy and decided to do to one last job, and his greed cost that Susannah lady her life."

Will stop stirring. "You lied about something else, didn't you, Claire?"

"I . . . I don't know what you—"

He said, "We know for a fact that Jamie had been dead for three days before that shed burned down."

"How . . . how . . . ?"

"Claire, where was your mother when the shed caught fire?" Will asked.

"It was like she told you. She'd set out in her gig to bring them chicken fritters to Father Donnelly."

"Do you think she might have had time to set the fire before she left?" Will asked.

"What?" Claire shook her head frantically. "No. No. It wasn't like that."

Will said, "You knew Jamie was dead all that time,

you had to have. You would have gone to the shed the next day to see if he'd left. You would have found his body, with a knife wound in the chest. Your mother had told him she'd turn him in if he stayed, but she knew that if she did that, it would become general knowledge that you'd sheltered a notorious criminal. Claire, I know your mother must have warned you to keep quiet about what happened, but—"

"Her mother didn't kill Jamie, Will," Nell said.

Will stared at her.

"He took his own life," she said. "Didn't he, Claire?"

The girl's eyes glazed over with tears.

"But you didn't want anyone to find that out," Nell continued, "because you knew about the Church denying Christian burial to suicides, and you thought people who weren't buried in the Church couldn't go to Heaven. That's why you told us he didn't feel guilty about Mrs. Cunningham, so we wouldn't suspect the truth."

Claire nodded, scrubbing at the tears spilling from her eyes.

"When did you . . . find him?" Will asked.

"The next morning," she said in a halting voice. "You know—after Ma kicked him out. He told her he'd be leavin' that night, and I reckon he meant it, but not how she thought he did—or how *I* thought he did. I shoulda known somethin' was up when he gave me the Sacred Heart. He told me it was for bein' a friend to him, but I knew what it meant to him. I reckon he figured he didn't need it where he was goin'."

"I reckon not," Nell said.

"I didn't sleep a wink that night," Claire said. "I missed him already, somethin' awful. First thing next mornin' I went back to the cranberry shed, kinda half hopin' he'd still be there, and I found him . . ." She drew in a tremulous breath. "He was layin' there facedown, but not on the quilt. He was on top of one of them pallets we store the crates and barrels on when they're full of cranberries, to keep 'em off the ground. There was blood all over the pallet, but that's not how I knew he was dead. I knew by the smell—and the flies."

Touching Nell's arm, Will said softly, "Are you all right?"

She nodded.

"I ran outside and fell to the ground and started screamin' and cryin'," Claire said. "I cried so long, my throat was sore and I could hardly see through my eyes, they was so puffed up. Anyways, I went back inside the shed to get him off that pallet and lay him down on his quilt. It was hard to lift him, 'cause he'd gone all . . . stiff like. But when I did, I seen the knife handle stickin' outa his chest. What he did was, he jammed it in between two strips of lath on the pallet so the blade was stickin' straight up. And then I figure he fell down on it."

Nell drew in a breath and let it out slowly. Will curled an arm around her waist.

"I got him on his back and pulled the knife out, and then I started draggin' him over to the quilt to lay him out all nice. That's when I saw the letters on the pillow, next to a stack of banknotes with some coins on top."

"Letters?" Nell asked.

"Yeah." Claire dug into a pocket of her skirt, sniffling. "There's a notebook and pencil in the cranberry shed, or was. It was for keepin' track of the different barrels and how long they been curin', and like that. He tore a couple sheets out and wrote a letter to me, and one to you. The one to you, I already mailed to Boston like he asked me."

She handed Nell a sheet of yellowish, lined paper folded into a badly rumpled little rectangle, saying, in a lowered voice and with a glance toward the house, "I keep it on me so Ma don't find it in my room." Nell unfolded it and found it to be neatly printed except for the signature.

Claire I am so sorry to make you find me like this. I know it is a sin to do what I am fixing to do but the good Lord knows how I runed my life. And ~~he~~ He knows about Susannah. I got my army tag round my neck so their will be no dout who I am. Claire would you please make sure I get a grave stone with my name and when I was born (Feb. 12th 1844) and when I died and a heart with a sword in it for repentence. And if you can please get this other letter to my sister Cornelia ~~Mur~~ Sweeney. She lives at 148 Tremont St. in Boston. This money is all I got. Take 3¢ for a stamp and would you please take a penny and go to St. Cats and ligt a candle for me. The rest is for the grave stone and if there is any left over it is yours to keep. Thank you for being a friend to me.

May God Bless You Always
James K. Murphy

"I still got the money," Claire said, "all but four cents for the candle and the stamp. It should go to you. I'll go fetch it and—"

"Keep it, please. I'll have the heart and sword added to his gravestone." Rereading the letter, Nell said, "He knew the Hewitts' address. He knew where I lived, but he never . . . He . . ."

"He was ashamed," Claire said. "He didn't want you to see him again till he had a real job and could hold his head up. He said he wanted you to be as proud of him as he was of you."

Tears pricked Nell's eyes as she returned the letter to Claire. She swallowed down the tightness in her throat, saying, "You *were* a friend to him. Thank you for that."

"So you got him laid out on the quilt?" Will said.

Claire nodded. "I covered him with the blanket and tucked it around him to keep the flies off, but I reckon it was too late for that. Then I started thinkin' about what would happen if I told Ma he killed himself. If she told the constables or if she didn't, it would of ended up the same. He would of been buried in the South Street Cemetery. That's where they put the paupers and them that don't have any family. And like you said, I thought if they buried him there, he couldn't go to Heaven. So I told Ma I'd been to the shed and he was gone. Which wasn't really a lie, 'cause he *was* gone, just not the way she thought."

"And she believed you?" Nell asked. "She didn't go there herself to make sure you were telling the truth?"

"I was bawlin' when I told her, and she could see from my face I'd been bawlin' all day, so she figured it was true."

"What did you do then?" Nell asked, wondering why she'd let Jamie's body lie there for three days.

"I went and made confession to Father Donnelly. He already knew about Jim bein' in the cranberry shed, but he couldn't tell no one, 'cause he learned about it in confession. So I went back to him and I confessed about Jim killin' himself and me tellin' Ma he was gone, which Father made me say Hail Marys over even though it wasn't a real lie, but he said it was. And he said self-murder was the kind of sin that meant you couldn't be buried in the churchyard, so I showed him Jim's letter, where he says he wants the heart and sword for repentance, but Father said that don't mean he repented the *suicide*. He said you can't repent somethin' you ain't done yet, else you wouldn't do it, and I said sure you could, but he said the Church don't see it that way. But priests can be wrong sometimes, 'cause they're just men, right? They talk to God, but they *ain't* God."

"Um . . . it's something like that," Nell said. No wonder Father Donnelly had been so reticent when Nell had asked him to bury Jamie in the churchyard. It wasn't Jamie's criminal activity that gave him pause; it was the suicide.

"I thought he'd understand," Claire said. "I thought he'd bury Jim in the churchyard 'cause he'd repented, but he said he couldn't, and then I knew I should of never told him how Jim died, but by then it was too late. So then, I didn't know what to do. St. Cat's is the only Catholic church around, so there wasn't no other priest I could go to. Jim was layin' there, and I couldn't let him be buried at South Street. I thought on it and thought on it, and finally, after a couple more days, I figured out what to do."

Will said, "You decided to burn the shed down so as to erase Jamie's true cause of death. That way, he wouldn't be regarded as a suicide, and could therefore be buried in consecrated ground."

"But Father Donnelly already knew that Jamie had taken his own life," Nell said.

"Yeah, but I figured since I told him that in confession, there'd be nothin' he could do about it. So I went back to the shed and took that knife and threw it in Mill Pond where nobody would ever find it. And that night, I said I was gonna go fix up the cranberry shed, but on the way there, I fetched one of them lamps from the barn that Ma don't want in the house 'cause they cause fires. I figured I'd open it up and pour the fluid on some of the crates and pallets, then light it on fire. But when I got in the shed, I wanted to take one last look at Jim."

Nell winced reflexively, knowing what her brother must have looked like at that point, given decomposition and the larvae. Will met her gaze gravely.

"I pulled the blanket off his face," Claire said, "and . . . God, it was . . . He was . . ."

"Yes," Will said. "We know."

"I think I screamed. I kind of stumbled back, into the cranberry sorter. It's metal, and when the lamp hit it, it cracked, I guess."

"And exploded as soon as the flame touched the camphene," Will said.

"All of a sudden, there was fire everywhere," Claire said.

"I take it the rest was as you told us before?" Nell asked. "Your skirt catching fire, and the bushel boxes in front of the door? Smashing the window to get out and running for help because you'd supposedly heard a man screaming?"

"I wanted the fire put out fast so there'd be . . . you know. Enough of Jim left to bury."

Will said, "What did your mother think when she came home and found out he'd been in the shed when it burned?"

"I told her I lied when I said he'd left, but not that I started the fire. Still, she was mad as a wet hen, let me tell you. She started wailin' on me somethin' fierce. But then she got real quiet and serious and said we had to tell the same story so I wouldn't come out lookin' like a . . . you know. A certain kind of girl. We had to both say we didn't know Jim had been hiding out in the cranberry shed, that I saw it was on fire and heard a man scream, just like I told the boarders, and that Jim must of died in the fire."

"But when you tried again to get Father Donnelly to bury him in the churchyard, he was still balky," Nell said.

"He said it didn't matter that he knew about the

suicide from confession, he *knew* about it, and he couldn't give Jim a Christian burial no matter if I'd made it look like an accident or not. It wasn't till you went and talked to him that he gave in."

It was a testament to Father Donnelly's humanity—and possibly his affection for Nell, whom he'd known since she was a baby—that he'd eventually agreed to bury Jamie in the churchyard with his family.

Claire said, "You know, I been thinkin' about it, and I think Jim knew all along what he was aimin' to do. Or he come to it early on, 'cause that first night, when I told him I'd bring him some things from the house—you know, the food and quilt and that—he asked me for a knife. He said he wanted it for whittling, 'cause he was bored. I said didn't he have a pocket knife? And he said yeah, but he liked a big knife for whittling, and would I make sure it was nice and sharp. So I brung him the knife, but I never knew him to whittle anything. I think he was just waitin'—you know—for the right time."

"I think you're probably right," Nell said, remembering what Claire had told them the last time they'd spoken. *He said I'd best know up front he was gonna be leavin' soon as the time was right, and that would be the end of us. I asked him was he gonna say good-bye or would I just come out there one night and find him gone. He said he was sick of good-byes. He'd had a whole lifetime of good-byes.*

Chapter 11

"WE'RE here, Nell," Will said softly.

Nell opened her eyes to find herself nestled against Will in the buggy, which he'd pulled up to the front of his parents' house. "I fell asleep *again*?"

"You've had a trying day."

"I thought you two would never get home." It was Viola's voice, coming from the front porch, where she and her husband were sipping the glasses of sherry they enjoyed every evening before dinner, she reading a book and her husband a newspaper.

Nell groaned softly as she realized Mr. Hewitt had seen her sleeping against Will's shoulder.

"We had to make an unplanned stop," said Will as he jumped down from the buggy and came around to Nell's side.

As he was handing her down, his mother asked him to join them for supper, as she did every afternoon—despite the fact that Will declined the invitation every time, so as not to have to share a dining table with Mr. Hewitt.

Will circled the buggy in silence. As he was climbing up into the driver's seat, he said, "Thank you, Mother. I believe I'd enjoy that."

He drove off to the carriage house with Nell, Viola, and Mr. Hewitt all staring after him. Viola met Nell's gaze with a look of surprised pleasure as her dour husband turned a page of his newspaper.

"Where is Gracie?" Nell asked as she climbed the porch steps.

"Eileen is getting her into her bathing dress for a little late-afternoon dip with the Palmer twins from down the road—Patty and . . . Polly?"

"Pammy," Nell corrected.

Viola said, "My dear, I wonder if you wouldn't be so kind as to take a look at the sketch I did this afternoon and tell me what you think of it. It's on my worktable in the greenhouse." She always called it "the greenhouse," although it hadn't been used for that purpose in many years.

"Of course," Nell said. "I'll do it as soon as I've washed off the dust of the road and dressed for dinner."

"You might want to look at the sketch first," said Viola with a meaningful glance at her husband, sitting with his head bent over the paper, his spectacles low on his nose. "I think you'll find it speaks to you."

O N Viola's worktable, amid the chaos of jars and brushes and paints, sat a large, thick envelope addressed to Mrs. August Hewitt, with no return address. Nell reached inside the envelope, which had already been slit open, and withdrew a sheaf of papers pinned to a letter engraved SILAS ARCHIBALD MEAD, ATTORNEY AT LAW. A smaller envelope slipped out and landed facedown on the floor. She bent to pick it up, freezing when she saw the address imprinted on the back: *Massachusetts State Prison.*

Duncan.

Mrs. Cornelia Sweeney was written on the front in Duncan's painstaking if untutored handwriting. Just her name, no address.

She turned her attention first to Mr. Mead's letter, which was written on thick, ivory laid paper.

Boston, August 19th, 1870
Miss Cornelia Sweeney, Waquoit, Massachusetts

Dear Miss Sweeney,—I beg to inform you that your petition for divorce from Mr. Duncan Sweeney has been granted by the Commonwealth of Massachusetts as of today's date. Enclosed please find the pertinent documents. Please be advised that I am in receipt of remuneration in full from Mrs. Hewitt for my legal services, which will explain the absence herewith of a request for payment.

After some initial reluctance on the part of Mr. Sweeney, of which you are already aware, he wrote to me earlier this week, advising me that he would not contest the divorce after all. I can only surmise that this change of heart was prompted by the letter you wrote to him, which I left with him when we spoke August 8th. I must admit that Mr. Sweeney's comportment during that meeting gave me little hope that he could be persuaded to cooperate. His having done so enabled the petition to proceed a good deal more speedily and efficaciously than otherwise would have been possible. Included with this correspondence is the enclosed letter, which he asked that I forward to you.

Also of considerable benefit, even more so than Mrs. Hewitt's acquaintanceships in high places, was your having been the instrument of Charles Skinner's expulsion from the Boston Police Department, which noble deed appears to have endeared you in no small measure to many an influential gentleman of this city. Would that I enjoyed such approbation myself. I daresay it would facilitate my professional endeavors to a very great degree.

As to Mr. Skinner, I enclose as well an article from the August 17th edition of the Boston Advertiser, *which I trust you will find of considerable interest.*

Should you require future services of a legal

*nature, I would consider it an honor to serve in
that capacity. Until then I remain,*

> *Your obedient and faithful servant,*
> *S. A. Mead*

Nell lifted the letter to find a newspaper clipping
pinned beneath it.

HOMICIDE IN A NORTH END DEN.

*A Former Constable Goes on a Rampage in
a House of Ill-Fame—He Is Stabbed to
Death by One of His Victims.*

About 11 o'clock last night CHARLES SKIN-
NER, a former Constable of the Boston Police Department assigned to Division Eight in the North
End, entered the bar-room of 103 Clark Street, a
shabby frame building that is one of the lowest and
most wretched brothels in that disreputable locality.
There SKINNER, who was well known as a ruffian
and a drunkard, made the acquaintance of MAGGIE
O'SHEA, a prostitute, whom he accompanied to a
curtained alcove on the second floor. Scarcely had

Miss O'SHEA drawn the curtain than SKINNER, who was in his usual state of inebriation, began abusing her in a most vicious manner. Upon hearing the assault, three females of similar stripe, MOIRA KELLY, BRIDGET DONOVAN, and KATHLEEN BRENNAN, flocked to her aid. SKINNER drew a large dirk-knife and ran a Muck in the confined space, threatening to kill them and wounding Miss BRENNAN and Miss O'SHEA. Being fearful of her life, one of the women struck SKINNER in the neck with a pocket knife, whereupon he fell to the floor, and in five minutes was dead.

The Police were summoned and took possession of the premises, but were unable to identify which woman wielded the blade, as all four denied having done so, just as they denied having witnessed the fatal stabbing. Inasmuch as the killing is deemed to have been a matter of self-defence, it is unlikely that any arrests will be forthcoming.

By all accounts, the deceased was in the habit of frequenting such establishments for the sole purpose of creating a disturbance and terrorizing the female inmates. His death has been greeted with jubilation in the North End.

"He who lives by the sword shall die by the sword," Nell murmured as she set the sheaf of papers aside and opened the envelope from Duncan, using a pointed palette knife.

Aug. 15th 1870, Charlestown State Prison

My Darling Wife,

Now don't be getting het up on account of me calling you that, it is the last time I will have the chance. Which I reckon is my own fault, who else's can it be? It sure is not yours. Father Daly says I brung it on myself and he is right. He is a Catholic preist Father Daly, not a Piscopal one like Father Beals may he burn in hell. It is about time they got a Catholic chaplan here even if he just got out of the seminery. He is not young though maybe 35, he was a prize-fighter before he took his vows and looks it.

Last week after that Mead was here I read your letter over and over, most of all the part where you say you forgive me which I never thought you would. You said it was a ~~wait~~ weight off your shoulders, well it is a weight off mine to. I couldn't think what to do so I gave the letter to

Father Daly in confesion which I hope you don't mind, he can't tattel about what he learns in confesion and he wouldn't, he is a good man. He asked me how did I make you lose the baby and I told him, and I swear I thought he would punch me preist or no preist. He said it must of been hard for you to forgive me and I said I reckoned it was. He said did I think it was right to let you be ruined after you shown such grace and I said no but the church don't allow divorce. And he said it is an offence on you're part not on mine because you are the one doing the divorce and I am the one it is being done to, and God will understand I didn't want it. I said if it is wrong don't God want me to fight it. He read you're letter again and he was quiet for a spell and then he said let it go. He said it is no sin so long as I don't marry again because that would be adultery. I told him you are the only wife I will ever want and I wish I could keep you but he said some times you got to take you're lumps.

Nell I hope he is a good husband to you that doctor, not like I was. I didn't mean to do what I done, but when I get angrey there is no telling

*what I will do and I reckon you had you're fill of
that.*

>God bless you and make you happy,
>Duncan Sweeney

Nell heard a girlish squeal and looked through
the rear wall of the greenhouse to see Gracie, in her
white swim dress, darting across the lawn toward
the beach with Eileen close on her heels; on the
sand in the distance sat her little towheaded playmates, waving to her.

"Where are you off to in such a hurry?" called
Will, striding toward her from the carriage house.

She hesitated, looking back and forth between her
beloved "Uncle Will" and her favorite playmates.

Will took Gracie's hand and told Eileen, in a
voice barely audible to Nell, to go on ahead, that he
would bring Gracie down to the beach in a couple
of minutes. Eileen walked away with Gracie straining in her direction as she tugged against Will's
grip. She said something to Will, pointing toward
the beach with a plaintive expression, as if every
second spent away from her friends were torment.

Will knelt on one knee, his back mostly turned to

Nell, his hands on Gracie's shoulders. Nell moved closer to the open back door of the greenhouse in a shameless attempt to eavesdrop, but he was talking too softly for her to hear.

Gracie nodded in a preoccupied way as Will spoke to her. She cast an impatient glance toward the beach, whereupon he gently cupped her face and turned it back toward him. She dutifully met his gaze and listened to what he was saying, her expression of forbearance gradually giving way to one of rapt attention.

She stared at him, her mouth opening. He stroked her braids.

Her eyes grew huge and shimmery; her chin wobbled.

She flung her little arms around his neck as he gathered her up, his face buried in the crook of her neck. Tears trickled down her cheeks, her mouth contorting in that way it always did when she cried, the way that broke Nell's heart.

Presently Will kissed her cheek and said something to her that made her laugh. He untied his cravat and wiped her tears with it, and then he spoke to her for a few more seconds, she nodding intently.

Glancing over his shoulder, Gracie noticed Nell

watching from the greenhouse doorway. She broke away from her father, who turned to look at her, his eyes gleaming wetly, as she raced excitedly across the lawn toward Nell. "Miseeny! Miseeny! Guess what?"

LATE that night, Nell, in her shift and wrapper, sprinted across the back lawn to the boathouse and climbed the stone steps. Lamplight glowed in the sitting room window, so she knew Will hadn't gone to bed yet, though she also knew there was a good chance he was sitting at the end of the dock, like last time.

"Please be Nell," he called from inside.

She found him sitting shirtless at the desk with his right arm in a washbasin, reading one of his medical journals. He set it down, smiling, as she approached. "It *is* you."

"How's your arm?" she asked, noting the items laid out next to the basin—gauze, shears, Epsom salts, silver nitrate solution, and a clean, folded towel.

"Hideous to look at, but with no sign of infection. Greaves is a bloody genius. I'm going to suggest he write an article about silver nitrate for the *New England Journal of Medicine*."

On the desk under the lamp was the letter Will had been in the middle of writing to President Grant when Nell and Cyril came looking for him Monday. He'd finished it, but had not yet mailed it, although it seemed to her he'd had plenty of opportunity, what with their trips into Falmouth these past couple of days.

She picked it up, skimmed it, and ripped it into pieces, which she dropped into his wastebasket.

"It took me days to compose that bloody thing," he said in a laconic, perhaps slightly amused tone.

Sitting on the edge of the desk, she said, "Your father is right, you know." August Hewitt had been stunned when Nell announced at supper that Will had been chosen to receive the Medal of Honor, and incredulous when she added that he was turning it down.

"He's not my father," Will said.

"He's still right."

It is a slap in the face of the president to refuse such an honor. For pity's sake, William. Have you no sense of propriety at all?

Sliding a baleful glance at Nell for having brought the subject up, Will said, *It's undeserved.*

Of course it's deserved, Mr. Hewitt had said as

he cut into his beefsteak. *The requirements are extremely exacting—I read about it in* Harper's. *One must have risked his life performing an act of the most extraordinary gallantry. At least two eyewitnesses are required. There is no margin for error. Why you balk at accepting it is beyond me.*

To Nell's knowledge, these were the first words August Hewitt had spoken to Will since his arrival at Falconwood. Viola had captured Nell's gaze across the dining table with a look of quiet astonishment.

"The only reason you feel unworthy of that award," Nell said, "is that you're mired in your old notion of yourself as flawed and undeserving. Frankly, I'm beginning to find that refrain fairly tedious."

"I've never known you to be quite such a pitiless shrew," he said as he lifted his dripping arm from the basin. "I find it captivating." As ghastly as the wound still looked, especially discolored as it was from the silver, it no longer showed any signs of redness or suppuration.

Pushing aside the basin, Nell scooted over on the desk, draped the towel across her lap, and motioned for him to lay his arm there.

"I do so love being tended to," he said as she carefully patted him with the towel.

Reaching for the scissors and gauze, she said, "You should have put yourself under the care of a physician the moment you got off that mail packet in Boston. What were you thinking, getting on a train and coming down here in that condition?"

"I *had* meant to remain in Boston and ask Foster to treat it. I was fairly confident I could trust him not to reach for the bone saw before he'd exhausted all other options."

"But . . . ?" said Nell as she packed the wound with gauze soaked in silver nitrate.

Will looked away with an uncharacteristically sheepish expression. "But my first evening in Boston, over drinks with Martin, he told me about you and Greaves."

"What did he tell you?"

"About seeing the two of you on the front porch the night before he came back to Boston. He overheard Greaves tell you that he would move to Boston to make you happy. And then he saw him kiss you."

"On the cheek. Did he tell you that?"

"He did. At that point, I was beyond mollification. What was I to suppose, except that he meant to make you his mistress? After all, you were both married, as far as I knew." He glanced at her and then away.

Bandaging the arm, Nell said, without looking at him, "I, um . . . I came here to tell you something that perhaps I should have told you earlier, but . . ."

"About filing for divorce from Duncan?"

Her head shot up.

"Greaves told me—this afternoon, before we left Packer's Mortuary."

"*That's* what you two were talking about?"

"Well, *he* was doing all the talking. He said something to the effect that I must not be quite the pig sconce he'd taken me for, since I'd finally declared myself to you—and that it was obvious you cared for me more than you would ever be able to care for him. And he told me that if my intentions were truly serious, this would be the time to do something about them, since you had a Boston lawyer working on terminating your marriage."

"Is that . . . all he told you?" she asked, thinking about the baby.

"Isn't that enough?" he asked with a chuckle.

"Why . . . why didn't you *tell* me you knew about the divorce petition?"

"For the same reason you didn't tell me you'd filed it." He smiled as her cheeks warmed. "You were hesitant to encourage the attentions of an incorrigible reprobate such as I. Good sense is nothing to be ashamed of, Cornelia. I've always respected your pragmatism."

"Oh, for God's sake." Leaning down, she took his face in her hands and kissed him, hard. He dragged her onto his lap and deepened the kiss, holding her so tightly that she could feel the pounding of his heart through her own chest.

"I love you," she told him as they drew apart, "deeply and madly and completely without reason. You must know that, especially after . . ." Her face grew even hotter, recalling their lovemaking the night before he left for France. "Surely you know I wouldn't have—"

"Of course," he said, enfolding her in his arms. "But I also know you're uneasy at the notion of throwing in your lot with me, as well you might be. I didn't want to put you in an awkward position by bringing up the divorce before you'd sorted things out. My intent was to convince you that I could be more than a vagabond cardsharp with a taste for the poppy, so as to encourage you to tell me about the divorce petition. But you've gone ahead and let the cat out of the bag ahead of schedule— proving you're not quite so clever after all."

"I mustn't be," she said, "or I would never tell you that the divorce has been granted."

"What?"

"As of the nineteenth, I am a divorcée. Makes me feel rather deliciously decadent, actually."

"Don't get used to the feeling, because I mean to make you a respectable married lady again as soon as you'll have me."

She pulled away to study his face, as if to gauge his sincerity. His eyes were dark and earnest. Threading his fingers through her hair to tilt her face up to his, he said, "I want you to be my wife, Nell. I've wanted it for so long, and I . . . God, I thought I'd have to spend the rest of my life wanting you, needing you, but knowing I could never have you. I'll do everything in my power to make you happy. I'll give you the kind of life you want, the kind you deserve. I swear to God I'll never touch a playing card again, or an opium pipe, or a morphine syringe."

"You don't believe in God," she said.

"I don't much care for religion. God is a different matter entirely. Gracie can come live with us, as she's always wanted. I'll sign that five-year contract to teach medical jurisprudence at Harvard."

"If you really wanted to teach, you would have been doing it all along," she said.

"You little nit. I love teaching, and I especially love the research—I just didn't love the agony of being in Boston, where all I could think about was you and how I could never have you. I appreciate your skepticism, though. You're not sure I've got what it takes to turn over a new leaf, and who could blame you? I know I have to prove myself to you, and I will. We can have as long an engagement as you like—two or three years, even longer if that's what you need."

"Oh, I need it to be quite a bit shorter than that," Nell said, a smile quirking her mouth. "A month or two, at the most."

Will's expression gradually transmuted from quizzical to stupefied. He lowered his gaze to her stomach, then looked up, his eyes huge.

"I assumed it wasn't possible," she said. "That's why I didn't think we needed . . . you know. Precautions. But it would seem you're right—I'm not quite so clever after—"

He pulled her close and kissed her for so long, she thought her heart would explode from joy. "I *am* going to make you happy, Nell, as happy as you've just made me." He kissed her forehead, her eyelids, temples, cheeks . . . "I'll build a house for you—for all of us. A palace—one of those absurd Back Bay monstrosities."

Nuzzling his prickly jaw, she said, "I'm actually quite fond of your house on Acorn Street."

"Then we can live there," he said between kisses. "But I want another house on the water somewhere, and a boat so I can take you out sailing, you and Gracie and the baby. Or sometimes just you and I."

"And we'll drop anchor at night, and swim naked under the stars."

"And dream about the future."

"And then we'll go home," she whispered against his lips, "and make those dreams happen."

Epilogue

From the Boston Advertiser, *October 15, 1870:*

A FELICITOUS WEDDING.

**DR. WILLIAM HEWITT MARRIED—
Medal of Honor Recipient and
Miss Sweeney United at King's
Chapel—President Grant Among the
Distinguished and Fashionable Guests.**

Rev. Martin Hewitt Officiates.

The wedding of Miss CORNELIA SWEENEY and Dr. WILLIAM HEWITT, which took place yesterday afternoon at 1 o'clock at King's Chapel, was one of the most notable events of the kind this season. It was a balmy autumn day, with bright sunshine, which was seen as an auspicious omen for the future happiness of the wedded pair.

Miss SWEENEY was born in the village of Falcarragh in County Donegal, Ireland, and brought up from an early age in East Falmouth, Cape Cod, where her father worked in the shipping industry; her parents are sadly deceased. A young lady of particular grace and beauty, she made the acquaintance of Dr. Hewitt through his parents, Mr. and Mrs. AUGUST HEWITT of this city, for whom she served, until her marriage, as governess to their adopted daughter.

Dr. HEWITT graduated from Oxford University before earning his medical degree at the University of Edinburgh. In 1861, he enlisted as an Army surgeon with the rank of major, distinguishing himself through extraordinary heroism at the Battle of Olustee before being captured by Confederate forces. He was held at the notorious Andersonville prison camp, from which he escaped in August of 1864. His most recent professional achievement is the establishment of a syllabus in medical jurisprudence at Harvard Medical School. It was for his service at Olustee that President Grant awarded him the Medal of Honor in a ceremony at City Hall Thursday morning. The groom was smartly attired for his nuptials in English morning dress with his Medal of Honor pinned to the breast of his coat at the urging of the President.

Miss GRACE ELIZABETH HEWITT, the 6-year-old child who has been the bride's charge, will henceforth reside with Dr. and Mrs. HEWITT, due to her attachment to her governess and the physical limitations of the elder Mrs. HEWITT. In two weeks' time, they shall all three, along with a small staff, board a private railroad car to San Francisco, where Dr. HEWITT will serve a yearlong guest professorship in forensic studies at the University of California's Toland Medical College. Upon their return to this city next autumn, Dr. HEWITT will resume his position at Harvard Medical School.

The church was decorated in the finest taste with baskets of flowers trailing a profusion of green creepers; the railings were likewise wreathed in beautiful flowers and vines. At noon, the carriages began to arrive, and the church to fill with ladies and gentlemen of the greatest elegance and distinction. In the second pew on the right sat President and Mrs. GRANT and Governor and Mrs. CLAFLIN, chatting together. Among the other close friends and family occupying the front pews were Mr. and Mrs. HARRY HEWITT; Mr. and Mrs. LEO THORPE; DENNIS DELANEY, aged 14, of Georgetown Preparatory Academy in Bethesda, Md., the ward of Superintendent of Pawnbrokers EBENEZER SHUTE; Dr. CYRIL GREAVES of Cape Cod; Rev. JOHN J. TANNER of Harvard Divinity School; and his sister-in-law, Miss REBECCA BASSETT. Other guests included Mayor SHURTLEFF, along with numerous members of the Board of Aldermen and the Common Council; Mr. and Mrs. WILLIAM ASTOR of New York; Judge and Mrs. HORACE BACON; Mr. and Mrs. ORVILLE PRATT; numerous colleagues and students of Dr. HEWITT'S from Harvard, including Dr. CALVIN ELLIS, Dean of the Medical School; and several members of the Hewitts' household staff, who were invited at the request of the bride.

Shortly after 1 o'clock, the bridal party arrived and Dr. HEWITT took his place at the altar with his best man, Dr. ISAAC FOSTER. First came the bridesmaids: Mrs. TANNER, Mrs. COOK, and the maid of honor, Miss EMILY PRATT, who is betrothed to Dr. FOSTER. The groomsmen were Mr. SHUTE and State Detective COLIN COOK. Det. and Mrs. COOK recently welcomed a baby daughter, whom they named CORNELIA after the bride.

The bride, who entered on the arm of playwright MAXMILLIAN THURSTON, wore a gown of white satin and point lace with a court train, a tulle veil secured by a wreath of orange flowers, and an exquisite diamond brooch in the shape of a sailboat, a gift of the bridegroom. She carried white roses and lilies of the valley. Miss GRACE HEWITT, in a dress of white silk illusion with blue satin piping and sash, a wreath of white rosebuds on her head, attended the bride as flower girl.

The ceremony was performed by the bridegroom's brother, the Rev. MARTIN HEWITT, who appeared toward its conclusion to be struggling with his emotions, as did the bridal couple themselves, the groom's parents, and several others in attendance.

At 3 o'clock Mr. and Mrs. AUGUST HEWITT gave a reception for their son and new daughter-in-law at their residence on the corner of Tremont and

West Streets. The parlors were festooned with roses, wreaths, palms, and flowering plants; a canopy was erected in the garden, where a small orchestra played. The festivities were formally launched with a series of toasts to the bride and the bridal couple, with perhaps the most touching, judging from the tears it inspired, being that offered by Mr. AUGUST HEWITT. The jubilant bride drank from a cup that was the wedding gift of Dr. GREAVES, a heavy silver goblet inscribed with the enigmatic legend: *To Higher Ground*.